FORBIDDEN GAME

CHICAGO RED TAILS
BOOK 4

SUSAN RENEE

Forbidden GAME

Cover art by Jack'd Up Book Covers

Editing by Brandi Zelenka, Notes in the Margin

Proofreading by Sarah Pilcher

Reader Team: Kristan Anderson, Stephani Brown, Jenn Hager, Jennifer Wilson

Formatting by Douglas M. Huston

❀ Created with Vellum

To Jennifer
Without your random TikTok going viral,
readers might not know about The Chicago Red Tails.
Beyond The Game would never have
become an international best seller
and my life wouldn't have changed for the better.
So thank you, Jennifer for being a loyal reader
who had no idea she would wake up one morning,
post a video, and change someone else's life.

PROLOGUE

RORY

Just tell me to S-T-F-U-A-T-T-D-L-A-G-G.

ME

D-Y-W-M-T-C-O-A-E-Y-P-T-Y-C-O-M-F?
😄 L-Y-H-F-M-L.

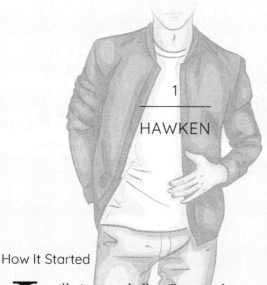

1

HAWKEN

How It Started

"I will rip your balls off, roast them over open coals, and shove them down your throat if you even think about touching my sister."

That was the warning Dex Foster gave the rookies at our very first practice. While I might not be a rookie, but rather a traded veteran, the seriousness of his facial expression causes me to avert my eyes to the floor as if his sister were standing in front of us all stark naked. She's not. She's not even here. In fact, there are zero women in this room at the moment.

So why is this a big deal?

"Ahh, don't be scared of this big bag of hot air," Colby Nelson tells us, his hands on Foster's shoulders. "His bark is always worse than his bite."

"Yeah, besides, Foster doesn't even like roasted nuts!" Zeke tells the group. "He likes his nuts a little salty."

Dex smirks. "Fuck you, Miller."

"Alright, alright." Colby raises his hand to settle us down. "Rookies, after practice today you each need to check in with Pam if she doesn't find you first for your promotional photos and all the shit that goes with that. Then get your asses over to Pringle's so we can socialize somewhere other than within these cement walls. Malone, you should probably check in with Pam too."

"Will do."

Thanks to it being a Monday evening, Pringle's Pub downtown isn't busy at all. Apparently, Nelson has an in with the owner because they have our entire team set up in the back of the bar.

"Hey man." Dex takes a seat next to me. "That was a great practice today. You can fuckin' play."

I'll take the compliment from Dex Foster. He's one of the best defensemen in the league.

"Thanks. Try to keep up next time, old man."

He barks out a laugh and clinks his glass with mine. "I'll do my best young whippersnapper. It's wading through all these young fuckin' egos that slows me down sometimes."

"Ah." I nod. "And here I thought it was a serious case of BDBP."

Dex's eyes narrow so I answer the question he doesn't ask.

"Big dick back pain."

He snorts this time and chokes on his drink. "Oh, shit.

Yep. That's totally what it is. And to make matters worse, I can't fit my back brace around my twelve-pack abs."

I give him my best sympathetic smirk. "I can definitely see how that would be a problem."

"I'm glad we understand each other."

I bring my glass to my lips. "Absolutely, eh?"

Dex shakes his head, a goofy grin on his face. "I think you and I are officially best friends."

"Finally." A young woman groans as she nudges Dex with her hip and waits for him to scoot over. "Take him off my hands, will ya?" She points at me. "But I warn you, he's no better than a room full of kindergarteners."

The girl that now sits across from me is dressed in what looks like some sort of yellow t-shirt dress with huge brightly colored flowers all over it, black tights or leggings underneath, and a pair of bright pink Converse shoes. I'm about to ask her what bag of skittles she came out of when she extends her hand.

"Rory Foster."

"Ahhh, the forbidden sister, eh?" I smile, acknowledging Dex's warning even though all I want to do is stare at her.

She's not the everyday basic bitch you see walking through town in jeans and boots with a pumpkin spice latte in her hands. She's unique, that's for sure.

Colorful.

I don't hate it.

The look makes me smile.

"I'm sorry," she says cocking her head. "What did you say?"

I gesture to Dex. "Oh, nothing. Dex just said—"

5

"Uh that you're a great sister to have around." He gives me a knowing glance and then clears his throat. "And it's nice to be able to look after you."

Rory rolls her eyes. "Please. Look after me. I think it's the other way around, brother."

"Okay maybe sometimes that's true," he answers. "But you're a good person and you deserve a good life. If I can protect you from all the sleezeballs out there, I will."

Rory turns back to me, her head pitching to the side. "Are you a sleezeball?"

"I'm Hawken. Uh, Malone. Hawken Malone." I shake my head, realizing that's not the question she asked. "Oh, uh no. No sleezeball here. I'm from Canada."

Dex scoffs. "Are you insinuating you're a nice guy simply because you're Canadian?"

"Absolutely. It's one of the things we're known for." I tick off on my fingers all the popular things about my home country. "Beautiful scenery, ice hockey, maple syrup, extreme politeness, and moose."

"And the word 'eh.' Eh?" Rory winks and fuck if my cheeks don't heat at the gesture, but I nod and give her a polite smile in return.

"Yeah. That too. Oh, and don't forget the cobra chickens."

Rory almost spits out her drink. "I'm sorry did you say cobra...chickens?"

"Yeah. Nasty fuckers."

"What exactly are cobra chickens, because I'm literally picturing a huge ass snake with feathers and a beak."

"Oh, sorry. No. That's creepy. I believe you would call them Canadian Geese."

She laughs. She's pretty when she laughs. Hell, she's pretty no matter what. "You mean a goose? You call geese cobra chickens?"

"Sure do. You might think they look cute and cuddly for a big bird but if you piss them off they will fuck you up. Hence the name cobra chickens."

"Oh, my God. Canadians are cool!" She and Dex burst out laughing. "So, you're new to Chicago then...eh?" she asks with a smirk.

Hell, she's cute.

"Yeah. Well, I've been here a few times for games in the past and I have dual citizenship thanks to my parents, but this is the first time I've lived in the States."

Rory leans across the table, her hand against her mouth even though Dex can still hear her. "Listen, if you ever need help navigating the city, call me. Don't trust anything Dex says. He'll totally lead you to the nearest whore house and he'll laugh while he does it."

Dex tugs her hand. "What are you saying about me?"

"Oh, nothing." She giggles and grabs his beer, taking a swig for herself. "Just telling our new Canadian friend here about your penchant for ridiculous pranks and how he should not trust a damn thing you tell him."

He chuckles. "Fuck you, Ror. You're not letting me have any fun."

"I teach my kids kindness, Dexter. Maybe you should sit in the next time we have circle-time."

"You teach?"

"Kindergarten." She nods.

Well, that explains the brightly colored outfit.

"That's great. How long have you been doing that?"

"This is year number three so not long enough for them to deplete my energy supply or turn me into a crotchety old cat lady."

I laugh. "Is that what happens when teachers retire in America? They become cat ladies?"

"Actually, in Chicago they probably become pigeon feeders. I guess I'll have to let you know in about..." She quirks her mouth as she thinks. "Thirty-ish years?"

I extend my hand to shake hers. "Deal. I'll be the old guy watching from my wheelchair in the park because my knees won't work anymore."

"Ah, yes. You and Dex both." She takes another sip of his beer, much to his dismay. "Where are you living anyway?"

"Anders Tower."

Her brows raise and she glances at Dex. "That's basically right next to us. We're over in the Lewis."

"You're both there?" I ask, wondering how on earth a schoolteacher can afford an apartment in that building.

"Well, Dex is there. He just lets me live there rent free because I decorate better than he does, I cook relatively well, and I'm the best sister in all the land." She waves her hand in front of my face like she's speaking of a magical place.

"Spoken like a true storyteller."

"Thank you very much." She smiles and gives a tiny bow. "For my next trick, I'll guzzle the rest of this beer and scarf down the biggest cheeseburger Pringle's has to offer because I'm fucking famished."

Dex shakes his head. "She's not lying either. I don't

know where she packs that shit away on that frame of hers. She's basically a stick."

Rory shakes her head. "A bundle of sticks you mean. I'm no twig. Plus, wrangling kindergartners all day is good cardio."

An attractive woman who is conversational, friendly, kind, has no problem tossing back a beer, and eats like a champ?

Fuck.

I like her.

How It's Going

"Alright, who brought the crocheted dildo?" Dex asks, holding up the pink penis shaped gift in his hand.

"It's not a dildo, asshat." I laugh, pulling it out of his hand and reaching for one of the new frying pans on the counter. "It's a potholder for the handle."

"Conveniently shaped like a penis."

"Of course. Made just for you from my brother," I tell him. "Remember I told you he knits too?"

"Yeah. You may have mentioned it once or twice."

"Well, he tried his hand at crochet and likes it even better. Plus, I thought Tatum might need some big dick energy over here occasionally."

Dex puffs his chest and narrows his eyes playfully. "Trust me. She's got all the big dick she wants anytime she wants it."

Shrugging, I let out a resigned laugh. "Well in that case, consider it your very own dick sock."

"What the fuck is a dick sock?"

Quinton speaks up. "You know...something to keep your dick warm. Like...like leg warmers, but for your dick. You're always telling us how tiny it gets when it's cold."

Dex's jaw practically unhinges as he glances nervously around the room. "I...do...NOT...what the fuck? My dick does not get cold."

"It won't now that you have a dick mitten," Colby states.

I nearly spit out my drink. "Dick mitten!"

"I don't NEED a di—"

"A dick muff?" Milo asks, glancing around at the guys, but I shake my head and point to Colby.

"I think dick mitten wins."

Dex sweeps his arms in a crossing motion in front of him. "Alright, alright. Nobody is wearing a dick mitten in this house. "

"Aww, come on Dexy." Tatum pouts, running her hand up and down his chest. "You wouldn't model it for me if I asked you to?"

His shoulders fall and he turns to goo right in front of our eyes. "You know I would do anything for you, babe."

It's unbelievable how smitten he is.

Both his girls have him wrapped around their fingers.

Three girls if you count Rory.

Speaking of, she steps up with her niece in her arms, passing her to Tatum and patting her brother's shoulder. "Lucky for you, bro, they're just potholders."

He holds it up one last time and wiggles it in front of my face. "How incredibly thoughtful of you. It's the perfect gift." His voice drips with sarcasm, which makes me laugh.

"Anything for you man."

"Thank you, Hawken," Tatum says, still giggling. "I love them."

"You're welcome."

"I love them too, Hawken," Charlee says. "Maybe I should put an order in with your brother."

Milo gives her a questioning glance and she shrugs. "What Honey? I was just thinking that I could cover one of my uh...you know...toys with it. How cute would that look sitting on your bookshelf?"

"Ooh not a bad idea," Carissa chimes in much to Colby's chagrin.

"Me too! I want one." Rory raises her hand. "Or maybe I need umm...six. No, seven! Can he do every color of the rainbow? I could do a ROY-G-BIV display!"

Seven?

Is she saying she has seven...toys?

She really has that many...?

Nope. Don't think about it Hawk.

This won't end well for you.

Dex throws his hands up to his ears. "LA, LA, LA! I don't need to hear my sister talking about her fuck toys! LA, LA, LA, LA, LA!"

Quinton mimics Dex's gesture shouting, "LA, LA, LA! Code PINK! Code PINK! Can't be hearing this! LA, LA, LA!"

Rory's mouth twists and she eyes Quinton. "Code pink? What the fuck is code pink?"

"I will rip your balls off, roast them over open coals, and shove them down your throat if you even think about touching my sister!" he shouts as if repeating an oath to a drill sergeant, his eyes squeezed closed.

His impersonation of Dex is right on point. Those are his words of warning to the team every year at the start of the season so the newbs on the team know not to go near Rory. Not that she can't handle herself. She's a fuckin' force to be reckoned with, but Dex has always been overprotective of his only sister. Shaking his head, Dex smacks Quinton's ass with his dick mitten and then gives him the finger with his other hand.

"Fuckin' right I will," he confirms with a smirk. He points at all of us as he turns himself in a semi-circle. "I know where all your dirty dicks have been and where they do not need to be is anywhere near my sister. I've watched you all at one point or another walk away with a puck bunny or two on your arm and if there's one thing my sister does not need in her life, it's horny hockey jocks who see her as nothing but a piece of meat."

Ooooh Dexter...

If ever there was a time I felt the need to cringe, this is it.

Rory's mouth opens and her eyes grow wide.

"Wait a damn minute," she says. "Are you telling me that code pink is some fucked up rule about me being off limits?"

Realizing his mistake, Dex shakes his head. "Rory it's not what you—"

"Are you seriously telling me that this is an actual thing? You tell the whole fucking team that they can't come anywhere near me?"

"It's not like that, Ror. I swear." Dex tries to save himself, but I don't see any way out for him in this case.

Rory places her hands on her hips. "Oh really? Tell me then. What exactly is your version of fucking code pink?"

Dex swallows nervously, looking to us all for help but none of us want to make eye contact. The women in the room though are genuinely curious and if I must say, a little perturbed.

"Ror, it's no big deal. Really," he starts. "I just..." He lowers his voice. "I know what you've been through before. I was just trying to—"

"To what, Dex? Huh? Make me out to be some monster freak nobody should go near?"

"No. Rory, I told you it's not—"

"You know I can take care of myself, right Dexter? I'm not your property. You don't get to choose who I spend my time with. I'm a fucking adult."

"I know you are. Look, we—"

"And correct me if I'm wrong, but were you not a horny hockey jock looking to get laid the night you met *and* slept with *and* knocked up the mother of your child?"

Oh shit.

She went there.

She turns quickly toward Tatum. "No offense, Tatum."

"None taken." She confirms with a nod.

An uncomfortable silence fills the room.

Yep. I'm certain we all wish we weren't here right now, but here we are. Standing in Tate and Dex's new kitchen while the two Foster siblings have it out in front of us.

"That was different."

"How so?" Rory crosses her arms huffing out a laugh. Tatum does the same.

"Yeah, how so?"

Dex's eyes flit between the both of them. "I was... helping her celebrate."

"Celebrate." Rory rolls her eyes. "Right. I remember now."

"Yeah. That's right. You know, new job, new home, new divorce..."

"New pussy hole to dip your stick in." She shakes her head. "You have some nerve asshole." Her expression remains stoic but I know her. She's hiding her feelings so she doesn't embarrass herself. I've been around enough now to know more about Rory than she may even know about herself. She tries to be the tough girl she thinks she needs to be, but on the inside, she's a sweetheart of a girl with real feelings who just longs to be loved and cared for. She wants the whole package.

She's a package kind of girl.

"That rule ends right now. If I want to fuck every guy on your goddamn team, you aren't going to say a word."

"But—"

"NO!" She puts her pointer finger up like she's reprimanding one of her kindergarten students. "You don't dictate who I see or who I don't see. You do not get a say, Dex. I don't answer to you. DO I make myself clear?"

"You're being unreas—"

"Do. I. Make. Myself. Clear?"

He sighs, relenting. "Yes. Fine. Whatever."

"I'm going to walk away from you now before I have to call a code black after smacking you in your teeny tiny nutsack with that penis covered frying pan!"

She abruptly turns and heads out the back patio door

toward the lake, and I hear Dex mumble, "My nutsack isn't tiny."

I was traded to the Chicago Red Tails from Vancouver a year after Dex had moved here. A brief history of playing against one another on separate teams, Dex was a defenseman, and a tough player who took the game of hockey very seriously. He could bolt down the rink faster than anyone I had ever seen, and his sharp eye and keen sense of direction helped keep pucks out of the net time and time again. Now here we are playing on the same team.

And now we're more than teammates.

We're friends.

The absolute best.

We've seen each other through the ins and outs and the difficulties of the game. We've mourned our losses and celebrated our wins together. We've bonded like brothers over the latest women in our lives, well, until Tatum came along.

Dex was smitten with her the moment he met her and that left me standing alone. Don't get me wrong, I'm ridiculously happy for Dex. He's grown a lot over the years I've known him and to see him dote on his little Summer and her mother who, I'm certain, will one day be his wife...he deserves every bit of happiness that has come his way. But on the other hand, Dex has always been my go-to person. These days I see more of his sister than I do him. Not that I'm complaining. Rory's a great girl with a fun personality and if she wasn't Dex's sister, AKA, the woman who would cause my balls to become disconnected from my body, I would want to see a whole lot more of her. She's smoking hot in her own unique way and I would be lying if I said her face hasn't crossed my mind at night when I'm digging through my spank bank.

But she's Rory.

She's my best friend's sister.

"I will rip your balls off, roast them over open coals, and shove them down your throat if you even think about touching my sister."

I guess what Dex doesn't know won't hurt him, because with the amount of time I've been in Rory's presence over the years, I've thought about it. I've thought about it more than I will ever admit.

2

RORY

Where the hell does he get off?

To think, all this time he's had some bull-shit rule about guys not hitting on me. No wonder none of them have ever given me the time of day. Not that I've asked for it or sought it out, but geesh, I was beginning to think something was hella-wrong with me.

I mean, besides the fact my brother is a star hockey player for the Chicago Red Tails.

As much as I love Dex and appreciate all he's ever done for me, his stardom hasn't won me any favors where my so-called friends are concerned. Or boyfriends for that matter.

Maybe I should just go home.

I'm sure I've made enough of an ass of myself in front of everyone that nobody is going to want me around. Least of all Dex and Tatum. I didn't mean to ruin their party but God, Dex can be a real asshole.

Plopping myself down on the grassy bank overlooking the lake, I stare out over the water watching the small waves lap at the pebbled beach below. Though there's a slight chill this evening, it's been unseasonably warm for this part of the spring. It's nice to finally get outside and breathe the fresh air.

Dex and Tatum were incredibly lucky to find this place. It really is the perfect spot for a home. The view from their living room gives off total lakeside vacation vibes, peaceful and calm. It's dreamlike. I could sit here all evening and never feel bored gazing at the water. It's one place I can be alone but never feel alone if that makes any sense at all. Whether I'm sitting here in front of the lake, or I'm staring at the ocean in places like Key West, I always feel like the water has some kind of magical quality that calms me when I'm near it.

I wonder how many dead bodies are in the water.

Loved ones never heard from again.

"There's got to be some way I could get away with murder."

"Whoa, Ror. If you're out here contemplating murder, maybe I should leave you alone."

I turn my face and find Hawken standing behind me, a beer in one hand, his other up in defeat. Rolling my eyes at his attempt at humor, I turn back to the water, drawing my knees to my chest and wrapping my arms around them.

"What do you want?"

"Can I join you?"

"I don't know. You better okay it with Lord Foster first."

He chuckles, but I don't find it the least bit funny.

"Why are you sulking?"

"I'm not sulking."

"You're sulking."

"Hmph!"

Lowering himself to the ground next to me, he nudges my shoulder with his. "Aww come on, Ror. He's not that bad. He loves you, you know."

"Yeah, he has a sick way of showing it sometimes."

"Cut him some slack. He's got a lot on his mind. New baby. New house. Busy playoff season. You know we might just pull it off this time. Then we'll really have something to celebrate in Key West this year."

"If you're here to make excuses for him, you can leave anytime."

"You're right. I'm sorry. No more Dex talk. Really, I just thought I would come check on you."

"Because Dex asked you to?"

"No. Because I wanted to."

I breathe in next to him and savor the scent of Hawken Malone. In all the years I've known him, he's always worn the same cologne. Aftershave? Who knows? Whatever it is, I've always liked it. Not that I would tell him that. It's some kind of earthy clean scent mixed with something fruity. Not like strawberry, fruity. Maybe pomegranate? Cranberry? Blackberry? I wish I knew. It's nice. I definitely don't hate it.

"Why? Do I look like a damsel in distress?"

His smile widens and that dimple I've seen many times before makes its appearance. He huffs out a laugh. "You? A damsel in distress? Hardly. But you're sulking." He gazes out at the water the same way I am. "If I'm being honest, you scare me sometimes."

That lightens my attitude a little. "Yeah?"

"Mhmm."

"How so?"

He lowers his beer bottle, placing it between his feet. "I don't know that I've ever seen someone be the most compassionate, fun loving teacher of small humans and also be able to cuss out refs the way you have for one."

I laugh. "Some of them don't know what the hell they're doing."

"You're this cute...energetic, creative person with some of the most amazingly fun fashion sense might I add, but you don't take anyone's shit either. You know what you want and you go for it." He shrugs, not making eye contact. "I think that's admirable."

Taking my gaze away from the water, I glance at my brother's best friend, who has also become my friend over the years. "You do the same, Hawk. You've always taken what you wanted. You're a master on the ice. Nothing ever slips by you. Everyone loves you."

"Everyone?" he asks, his eyes falling down my body before catching my stare. For a minute I wonder if he's asking about me, but I've never given him any indication of my feelings toward him one way or another.

Because he's Dex's teammate.

He's Dex's best friend.

Dex.

Dex.

Dex.

I could tell him that I've always thought he was attractive. I could tell him I had a crush on him when he first joined the team. I could tell him I've diddled myself with his face in my brain a few times in my life and that I've even nicknamed one of my toys The Hawk because of him.

But I won't tell him a thing.

Because he belongs to Dex.

As does everyone else I know.

"Uh, I've seen you in bars after games, Malone." I roll my eyes, thankful it's getting darker outside and he won't notice. "You've literally been able to pick up any girl you want. Sometimes more than one at a time, although let's not even get into that discussion. I do *not* want to know."

"You think I'm proud of that?"

"Are you seriously trying to tell me you're not?" I scoff. "I'm not naïve you know."

"No, you're not. But you are wrong."

"Mmkay."

He huffs quietly beside me, shaking his head. "You know, contrary to the man-whore you must think I am, that's not the life I want for myself."

"Yeah? Then why do you do it?"

"Because I'm a man who sometimes can't help himself. A man with a lot of pent-up adrenaline after a game and if that's the only way to relieve it...my sex life doesn't embarrass me, Rory."

"Ugh, can we please refrain from further conversations about your sex life?"

"Sure, but you started it." He takes a swig of his beer.

"If it's not the life you want for yourself, then what do you want?"

He's quiet for a minute before he answers. "I want... this." He gestures around us. "I want a big house in a quiet spot away from city life. I want to be able to come home to someone who wants me."

I cock my head. "Hawken, everybody wants you. I'm one hundred percent certain on any given day if you skate out on the ice with a sign that says please date me, every woman in the arena would be lined up. Carissa and I would spend an entire day just writing down all their names."

"And that's the problem," he mumbles.

"Huh?"

"Do you think any of those women would want me for who I am off the ice? Because all I ever see are the ones wanting to take my dick for a ride in hopes I'll date them and share my celebrity status. Or they just want to post about it on social media. So, when you ask what I want, Rory, what I want is this. Peace. Happiness. Somewhere to come home to where random women and reporters with cameras aren't up in my shit twenty-four-seven."

The more he talks, the more I find it hard to swallow. The very thought of random women taking his dick for a ride repulses me and sends a quick stabbing pain through my upper body. I don't like it. I push my fist into my chest trying to ease the discomfort.

"Okay, so why don't you buy yourself a house out here then?"

"Because."

"Because why? Seems like a damn good idea, don't you think? If you want peace and quiet, Hawken, then take it. It's not like you can't afford it."

He draws a deep breath, releasing a long sigh. "Because for as much as I relish the peace and quiet sometimes, being out here on my own would be lonely. I would spend way too much time up in my head and that's not healthy either."

"You're alone in your penthouse."

"That's different."

"How so?"

He shrugs innocently and picks at the grass between his feet. "I don't know. The city distracts me. I can't hear much, but the city lights, the traffic, the sirens...even if it doesn't always sound loud, living in the city feels...busy. I don't feel so lonely. Plus, up until recently, I had you and Dex right next door."

"That's true. I'm sorry your best friend won't be so close anymore. But you know you're still welcome to come hang out any time."

"Yeah?"

"Sure. It's not like I have much of a life beyond lesson planning and watching the Food Network. Who knows how many people my brother has warned against coming near me. He may as well put up a billboard."

Hawken chuckles softly. "I really don't think it's billboard bad but thank you for the offer. Maybe we can still have pizza night once in a while."

"Hell, yeah. God knows, I can't eat one of those suckers by myself. If Dex isn't going to be there, I'll need someone with a strong metabolism to help me out. Besides, if I'm going to find you a partner, I'll need to know all your eccentricities.

Fuck. There's that feeling in my chest again.

"I'll tell you anything you want to know. Any prospects come to mind?"

I shake my head. "No but give me time. I'm sure I can come up with someone to hook you up with that you haven't already impaled."

He gives me an annoyed side eye. "Very funny Rory."

"Ooooh look who's irritated now? I'm rubbing off on you tonight."

Aaaand now I have to be done because the only thought dancing through my head at the moment is what it would be like to actually rub myself off on Hawken Malone.

"Uh, if you'll excuse me," I murmur, pushing up from the ground. "I need a potty break." I turn back before I head to the house and lay a hand on his shoulder. "But thank you...for the chat."

His eyes reach mine and he smiles at me. It's not the everyday brotherly smile I get from him when he's hanging around Dex or the guys. It's softer, vulnerable.

"Anytime."

I return his smile and step off toward the house to clear my head of all things Hawken.

"Potty break...and maybe a stiff drink."

"Miss Foster, thank you so much for helping us put together this year's PTO carnival. Your ideas and attention to detail are immeasurable." Mrs. Anderson, our PTO President squeezes my shoulder. "I seriously don't know what we would do without you."

"Oh, you're welcome. It looks like the weather is supposed to be great too so hopefully we have a great turnout."

"I hope so," she says. "This is usually our biggest money maker. Especially with your connection to the Red Tails.

"And with the soon to be Mrs. Foster on our team too, how can we go wrong?" Her smile widens and her eyes sparkle. "I'm seriously already fangirling a little over our local celebrities. We are so lucky to have them in our community."

"Is your brother doing the dunk tank again this year?" one of the moms asks, checking over her notes.

"Yep. Planning on it. And Zeke Miller will be here running the slapshot game. And Colby Nelson will be running the Plinko Puck Drop. They were all just saying the other day that although it's playoff season and they shouldn't be doing too much extra in between games, they love hanging out with the little kids. And since two of them are dads now, you know, they're into this kind of casual fun. It's a safe way for them to give back."

Mrs. Anderson laughs. "Well, please thank them for us again for being such willing participants."

"Will do. I think the team is also planning to donate merch to give away as prizes. Cups, hats, t-shirts. That kind of thing. The team's social media marketing rep is a good friend of mine and she's married to Colby, so she'll get that together for us. She'll be here that night too if that's okay. She'll want to get some promotional video to use for the guys."

"That all sounds great! I really appreciate it."

"Sure thing. It's just as good for them as it will be for the school."

"Wait till my husband hears that some of his favorite players will be there," one woman says with a laugh. "I bet suddenly an elementary school carnival will be the most important event on his calendar."

Several of the other moms laugh and I smile right along with them.

I suppose if I'm good for anything, it's getting professional hockey players to come help raise money for little kids.

That's got to mean something, right?

The alarm on my phone dings reminding me of the other engagement I have tonight. I close my binder and grab my things as my friend and colleague Shelly leans closer to me.

"Hot date or something?"

I roll my eyes. "I don't know about hot, but yeah. I do have a date."

Her brows pop up. "Oooh do tell."

"Some guy I met at Pringle's last time I was there with Tate. He asked for my number and I gave it to him."

"Wow! I'm impressed. Look at our little Rory putting herself out there."

"Yeah, yeah. Anyway, I've got to get home and get ready. I'm meeting him in an hour."

"Good luck!"

3

HAWKEN

"Alright gentlemen, you looked good out there today but we have to remember to remain focused at all times." Coach Denovah makes eye contact with each one of us. "Round one was easy. You barely had to work for it, but don't let your egos get in the way when round two starts. If you want the win bad enough, and by God, after the work you've all put in these past few years, you deserve it, you've got to give two hundred percent. You've got to push back the moment you're challenged. This ice belongs to you. This game belongs to you. The win belongs to you. So fucking take it."

The team rallies together and then we're dismissed from the ice with a stern word of caution from Coach not to do anything stupid before the second round of playoffs starts in a few days.

"He acts like we won't be right back here on this ice tomorrow morning," Dex mumbles with a laugh as we head off the ice and down the hall.

"Nah." Colby shakes his head. "That's just the way he's always been."

"I don't know about you guys but I'm ready to kick some second-round ass." I stash my stick on the rack and head into the dressing room to get out of this uniform, the guys following behind me. We're one round closer to taking it all this year. It's ours to lose as far as I'm concerned.

"Me too, bro, but first I'm ready to go home and *get* some ass." Dex wags his brows to the laughter of the rest of the guys, and I simply shake my head.

"You're a horn ball, dude."

"Yep. Just the way my girl likes it."

QUINTON

I just got a DM from some chick asking me to tell her what I would do to her. What the fuck? I don't even know who this woman is. Women have balls these days.

ME

Tell her you would shove a butt plug in her and then order her to make you a sandwich.

COLBY

LOL! But tell her to keep it down because Ted Lasso is on. #barbecuesauce

ZEKE

GIF of Roy Kent saying, "Fucking Hell"

QUINTON

Hmm...I think my sandwich is missing
something but I can't put my finger on it.

DEX

If you put your finger on it, she'll come.
Guaranteed.

ME

Better find some Sriracha. That's
obviously what the sandwich is missing.
Also, has she come yet?

QUINTON

With stuffed face Hmm? Oh yeah. Twice
now. She came so hard the second time
around, she farted and the butt plug shot
across the room. Broke a window and is
now rolling down Lake Shore Drive.

DEX

Oh Fuck! I just spit out my protein shake!
😂

QUINTON

Also, FYI—best fuckin' sandwich I
ever had.

ME

But did you get to see her titties? It's
no fun if you don't get to see her titties.

DEX

In case you were all wondering, Hawk's a
boob man.

ME

Damn straight. Women's titties are God's
gift to men.

COLBY

Where's Milo?

DEX

LAAAAAANDRIC!

MILO

Powers down his motorboat Yessssss?

COLBY

Motorboat? Is that code for cock ring? Did Charlee get you a new cock ring buddy?

DEX

Pics or we don't believe you.

MILO

No. I was literally motorboating my wife, Asshat. #ilikeboobstoo

ZEKE

I haven't seen titties up close in longer than I care to admit. 😟

COLBY

Don't worry buddy. We'll get you back there.

ZEKE

It's all good. Pussy is much better anyway.

DEX

Mmmm pussy.

QUINTON

I do enjoy a sweet vagina.

ME

cringes and looks at everyone else Did he...did he just say...vagina?

DEX

He did, indeed.

ZEKE

Dude, what medical textbook did you skidoo out of?

QUINTON

What? That's what it's called, isn't it?

ME

Bro, you call it anything other than vagina. Nobody likes the word vagina.

MILO

Pussy, cunt...snatch.

COLBY

Twat (that was Carissa's). I prefer honey pot myself.

MILO

Charlee just said honey pot is sooo historical romance. Well done Colby.

COLBY

bows

DEX

Panty Hamster, pink taco, poontang...

ME

Fur burger. Cream pie. Hot box.

DEX

Fairly sure we could be here all night.

> **ME**
> *nods*

> **MILO**
> Maybe you should just put your phone down for the night, bro. Go watch some porn.

> **QUINTON**
> *high fives Milo* Yes, Daddy.

I reread this entire text conversation and laugh all over again, tossing my phone onto the couch next to me. If anyone other than us guys were to ever read our convos, they would think we're all a bunch of perverted nutsacks.

Probably because we are.

I lean my head back on the couch, releasing a deep breath and trying to decide what to do with myself for the evening. This is one of those nights that reminds me of my conversation with Rory not too long ago about being lonely. With Dex and Tatum now living lakeside, I can't just barge into their penthouse anymore and hang out. I suppose I could see what Rory's up to tonight, but she has her own life. It's not my place to ask her to entertain me.

Though now that visions of her entertaining me are swimming through my mind...

Staring at the blank screen of the television in front of me, I go through the motions of turning it on and as if my fingers know what to do I scroll to the only channel I tend to watch as often as ESPN. Lucky for me, the woman with huge titties being fucked in the shower has dark hair just like Rory. Turning the sound down lest anyone in this building ever catch me watching porn, I lay the remote next to me and slip my hand down inside my sweatpants.

"Why the fuck not?"

With my hand on my junk, I watch the couple in the shower go at it against the tile, their bodies slapping together, her head tilted back with his hand around her neck as he grunts to her.

"Yeah, you like this cock...take my cock Angel. Take it all."

Her moans and the bounce of her tits as he impales her body are what keep my attention the most. My dick stirs in my hand and I give it a squeeze right at the base, imagining myself inside her instead of him.

Knock, Knock, Knock

"Son of a bitch."

Grabbing the remote I power off the television, reluctantly adjust my chubbie, and then head for the door.

"No, Mrs. Golland," I say as I open the door. "I haven't seen any ghosts in the el—Oh...hey." My brows furrow. "What are you doing here? What's wrong?"

I don't think I've ever seen her look so defeated.

And so beautiful at the same time.

"Rory?"

She blinks up at me and tears trickle down her face. "Can I come in?"

I don't even hesitate. I kick my door open and pull her inside, doing the quickest assessment I possibly can of her.

"What's going on, Ror? Are you hurt? What happened?" I gently cup her face in my hands. "Hey, look at me."

Her makeup is smudged, but she finally reaches my

gaze. Her beautiful copper-colored eyes are now red-rimmed. "Talk to me, Ror."

"Sometimes I regret being related to my brother," she says with a trembling chin.

"Why? Did he say something to you?"

She shakes her head. "No, but he doesn't have to, to profoundly impact my life."

"Why is that?" My brows pinch together. "I'm sorry, I'm not following."

"I was on a date," she blurts.

She's dating someone?

Shit.

I don't want to talk about this.

"Okay...do you want to talk about it?"

Please say no. Please say no. Please say no.

"It was some guy I met..."

Ugh. We're talking about it.

"He took me out and while we were eating, he asked if I was related to Dex and once I told him I was, because duh, I'm sure he did his homework and already knew I was related, he couldn't stop talking about hockey and the Red Tails and how great Dex Foster is and how Dex is his favorite player blah blah fucking blah."

She sighs and then tosses down her purse and kicks off her shoes. An act that inwardly makes me smile because I like that she's comfortable here.

"I mean, yeah, I like hockey. I don't mind talking about it. Clearly whoever I end up with in life is going to have to love hockey at least half as much as I do, but then he..." She stops in her tracks and bows her head. "You know what? Never mind. Doesn't matter."

"What doesn't matter?

"It's nothing."

"Rory, it's not nothing. You're upset. Your feelings matter. You want to sit? I'll get you a drink. You want some chocolate milk?"

She stares at me, her eyes brightening. "You have chocolate milk?"

"Of course, I have chocolate milk. Are you kidding?"

"Since when? You don't like chocolate milk."

I shrug. "Since it's your favorite drink when you're having a bad day, so I always keep chocolate syrup in my fridge."

Her shoulders fall and her chin trembles again. "You do that for me?"

"Yeah. I mean, it's no big deal. So, is that a yes to the chocolate milk then?"

She nods.

"Good. Now tell me what doesn't matter that clearly matters even though you're pretending to want to drop it when really, you need to talk about it so you can get it all off your chest."

Because I know you, Rory.

She sits on my couch while I head into the kitchen area and pull the milk out of the fridge. I'm just grabbing a glass from the cupboard when she says, "So we were um...you know, making out in his car and..."

Noooo no, no, no, no. I don't want to hear this.

"He felt me up and..."

Fuck. Shit. Dammit. Fuck!

"Then he said, 'Is this enough to earn me a ticket to the

next playoff game? Think you could introduce me to your brother?'"

"What the..." Shocked at her story, I drop the glass I was holding and jump back as it hits the floor and shatters.

"Fuck."

What kind of an asshole would treat Rory that way?

"Are you okay?"

"Yeah. Fine, sorry," I reassure her.

I'm so not fine.

I'm fucking pissed at that guy.

"Just dropped a glass."

If he were here right now, I would kill him.

Knock his fucking head into the wall.

And then push him out the goddamn window.

Opening the pantry on my left, I grab the broom and dustpan and sweep up the broken pieces of glass and toss them in the trash. "That guy's a fucking douche Rory. I'm really sorry."

"It's not like this was the first time." She shakes her head. "And I guess it won't be the last."

"You mean this has happened before?"

She nods.

"How many times?"

God, I don't know why I need to know, but I fucking need to know.

"Every time. Every relationship."

My chest hollows at her confession and for a fleeting moment I want to throw something across my living room in a fit of rage for her.

"This has been my whole life, Hawken. My last real, well, what I thought was sincere relationship, ended after I had just slept with a guy who then said to me, and I quote, 'Phew that one was season ticket level good. Or maybe even just a good seat by the ice?'"

"Fuuuucking mother fuckers." It's the only thing that comes out of my mouth because I can't ask her to take me to the houses of every guy she's ever been with so I can beat the living hell out of them for treating her like absolute shit.

Grabbing another glass, I quickly mix up some chocolate milk for Rory and deliver it to her.

"Every guy I've ever been with. They all know or find out I'm related to Dex Foster, superstar defenseman for the Chicago Red Tails, and just like that, I become their steppingstone to get to him. And it's not just men. I've lost many female friends over the years who only hung out with me to try to get Dex to notice them." She sighs. "Thank you for this, by the way."

"You're welcome." I silently take a seat next to her and let her pause to take a sip. Which is really just me pausing to wrap my head around everything she's told me.

"Mmmm yes. It's so good."

As much as I love watching her enjoy her drink, she needs to cut that shit out before my chubbie comes back. I cannot be thinking about Rory that way. Especially not now.

"You seriously make the best chocolate milk. Better than the store-bought kind."

"It's all in the wrist."

"It is?"

"I don't know." I smirk. "I just made it up."

She takes a moment to drink a few more sips, wiping her face with the back of her hand. It's cute.

"It's just..." She sighs. "Why can't people just like me for me? Why is everyone so fucking obsessed with Dex? Why can't I find someone who enjoys the sport but doesn't care who I'm related to?"

You know, I think I might know a guy.

"Shit, Rory. I...I'm sorry," I tell her, shaking my head. "You don't ever deserve to be treated that way and it's pissing me off that all those low-life assholes didn't see you for who you are. I wish I had the right words to say right now. Does Dex know about all this?"

"Yeah. He found out when the last relationship ended because I came home in a fit of tears. Consequently, the ex was black balled from the arena for any Red Tails home game for two straight seasons."

"That's a start. But it's not enough."

She shrugs. "It is what it is. Clearly, we weren't meant to be. Dex was pissed of course, and then he felt terrible that this has been my life. He tries so hard to look out for me, you know?"

"He really loves you."

"We're all each other has. Well...had. Now he has you guys...and Tate."

"But who do you have, Ror?"

Her gaze turns downward. "I have Dex. And Tatum and my friends at work. And Carissa and Charlee because they're already married to hockey players, so I don't have to worry about them wanting my brother."

She tries to laugh but I see right through her. She's hurting.

"Hey. Come here." Wrapping an arm around her, I pull her into a side hug. "You have all of us, alright? The whole team would be there for you in a hot minute if you needed us. You know that, eh?"

"Yeah." She sinks into my side and for the first time ever, tiny nervous flutters erupt in my chest. She feels good against me like this. I think I like it. Instinct has me wanting to kiss the top of her head, but I stop myself before I cross that line.

"So, what did you do? With your date tonight, I mean."

She huffs a quiet laugh. "Well since he had his hand up my shirt, I grabbed his dick, gave it a squeeze, and laughed."

"Oooh." I cringe teasingly. "You got him right where it hurts."

"Hell yeah, I did. I told him it wasn't nearly big enough to gain access to the arena—mine or Dex's and he could kindly fuck all the way off and lose my number. Then I hopped out of his car and came here."

My brows shoot up as I glance down at her. "You walked here?"

"Yeah. We were just a couple blocks away. I knew I didn't want to go home to an empty penthouse so I came here hoping you were home. I'm sorry. You're the closest thing I have to a friend nearby."

"Closest thing to a..."

What the fuck?

I pull away from her so I can turn and see her whole face. "Rory, I *am* your friend. We're friends. You know that. You're always welcome here."

"Thanks, Hawk." Her smile is faint but it's there. With a nudge to my shoulder, she lifts her glass. "And thanks for the chocolate milk. You always know how to make me feel better."

"It sounds like you took care of this one all on your own. I'm proud of you. But I'm also sorry this is something you've had to go through. You don't deserve to be treated like you're second best. You're a great person, Rory."

"Yeah well, if you could just...you know, tell that to all the non-douchey single guys out there in the world..."

Not a fuckin' chance.

"I'll do what I can, eh? You'll find someone who makes you happy and gives you the world. I have no doubt." I watch as she drains the rest of her milk. "You want another one?"

"I shouldn't."

"Fuck that. Do you want one?"

Sheepishly, she gives me her sweetest puppy dog eyes and nods.

I smile back at her. "Coming up. You want to hang for a bit?"

"Did you have plans tonight? I'm sorry I shouldn't have shown up unannounced."

"Nonsense. It's all good." I rest her glass on the counter and grab the milk and chocolate sauce again. "I'm free."

"Can we just watch some T.V. or something?"

"Whatever you want. Remote is on the coffee table."

I finish mixing up her chocolate milk and grab a bottle of water for myself.

"Wow!"

"What?"

I look out at Rory from the kitchen island. Her brows are perched high on her head.

"She's really gettin' railed! From both ends even!"

"Hmm?"

Oh shit!

My face falls when I realize what she's talking about.

"Fuck! Shit! Rory, fuck. Sorry!" I'm a clusterfuck of a hot mess as I practically leap into the living room area, tripping over myself and tossing my bottled water to the couch. Surprisingly not covered in spilled chocolate milk, I place her glass in front of her before grabbing the remote and hitting any button that gets us away from what I was watching earlier.

But she giggles as her smile widens. "Oh, this is muuuch better!"

"What?"

I turn around to see a dude being fucked in the ass by another dude, my ass clenching of its own accord in response. "Shit. Oh, God. Sorry, Let me..." I hit the button again several times but it's the wrong fucking button and now the sound of two guys fucking flows through my surround sound. Skin slapping and mumbles of 'so fucking deep. Yeah. Take my cock, take it' ring out through the room.

Rory is a bundle of laughs and cackles watching me try to get rid of the porn on the screen with her in the room.

Fucking Christ, this is embarrassing.

Finally, I hit pause so I can get my bearings and focus on the damn buttons. Rory points to the screen.

"Now that one would've gotten season tickets and its own personal suite." She whistles. "Whoa! Look at the size of that thing."

I cringe because fucking hell, she's marveling at a dick in front of me and it's not mine.

"I'm not looking at anyone's dick Rory."

"Yes you are." She nods, pointing. "Look at it!"

"No."

"Turn around and look," she giggles.

"Not a chance."

"What's the matter? You scared his dick might be bigger than yours?"

"He works in the porn industry Rory. I'm sure that means his dick is..."

She tilts her head. "Is what?"

I shake my head. "Don't make me say it."

"His dick is what, Hawk? You have to say it now. I'm not letting it go."

With a roll of my eyes, I stare at her and say, "Girthy. His dick is probably girthy."

She cackles. "I just wanted to hear you say girthy about some other man's dick."

"You know I see dicks every day, right?"

"Obviously. How many hours a day do you watch this stuff, anyway? Maybe you should make popcorn. Porn and popcorn." She claps her hands excitedly. "This night just got so much better!"

"I meant in the locker room, Ror. I see dicks in the locker room every day. It's not a big deal."

"You mean yours isn't a big deal?"

"Oh." I scoff out a laugh. "Mine is a huuuuuge deal."

"That's not what Dex says."

"Fuck Dex. He wishes his was as big as mine."

She smiles. "Just kiddin'. He doesn't talk about dicks."

"Yes, he does. Just not with his sister."

"Fair," she agrees with a slight bob of her head.

"And we're not watching porn together. No way."

"Aww come on," she pouts. "Where's your sense of adventure?"

"Sorry, babe. I don't mean to bring up your brother. I really don't. But if he knew I was watching porn with you at night he might yank my dick right off and shove it down my throat and if you don't mind, I'm a little uh, attached to my dick and would like it to remain right where it is."

She twists her mouth and narrows her eyes before she finally relents. "Okay what else d'ya got?"

"How about *Ted Lasso*?"

"Ooooh!" Her eyes light up. "Can we watch the Christmas episode?"

"It's only the best episode of them all, eh? So, yes."

She snuggles into the couch, bringing her legs up to her chest. "Okay. Let's do it."

I toss one of my many fleece throw blankets over her. "Here. I know how you like to snuggle."

"Thanks, Hawk. And for what it's worth, thank you for making me laugh. I really needed it."

I give her my best reassuring smile. "You're welcome. I'm glad you stopped by."

But oh, my God, I will never speak of this night to Dex. Ever.

4

RORY

"Hey Rory." Carissa walks over after taking a few pictures of the complete set up and lowers her voice. "I have all the guys set up in their stations, but I haven't seen your brother yet. He hasn't messaged you, has he?"

The entire blacktop area of the elementary school is set up like one big carnival. Around the outer edge of the lot are two rows of game booths with everything from ring toss to balloon pop to the dunk tank at the end. Zeke is ready to go with his slapshot net and Colby is already playing around with his Plinko Puck Drop game. On the other side of the pavement sits a bake sale tent, popcorn and cotton candy tent, a refreshment stand, and three different food trucks.

I look over toward the dunk tank and find it empty.

"Dammit Dex!" I murmur, yanking my phone from my back pocket to check for any missed texts. "We open in ten minutes!"

When I see there are no texts from him, I send him one in hopes he'll tell me he's almost here.

ME

Where are you bro? We open in ten!

DEX

Ooooh shit! Ror! I'm so sorry! I completely forgot about it. Tatum isn't feeling well so I took Summer out for a bit and now she's napping. I don't think I'm going to be able to get away. Rory I'm so fuckin' sorry to let you down!

Ugh. How can I be mad when my friend isn't feeling well and he's with my niece? I can't blame him there.

ME

Don't worry about it. I'll figure it out. I hope Tatum is okay.

DEX

Stomach's queasy and she has a headache. Maybe some bad sushi. She's sleeping too. I'm sorry!

ME

It's okay. I'll handle it.

"Did you guys bring all the prize merch or did Dex have that?"

Carissa nods. "We have it." She looks toward Colby's SUV. "Looks like Colb and Zeke are handling it now."

"Great. Dex isn't coming. Tate's sick so he's with Summer."

"Aww I hope she's okay."

"He said something about bad sushi. But fuck..." I

bring my hand to my forehead. "What do I do about this dunk tank? It's our most popular thing at the carnival. Especially the way Dex plays it up with the kids. They love it."

"I could have Colby or Zeke step in if you want," she offers.

I almost take her up on her proposal, but another idea pops into my head. "Hold that thought for just a minute. Let me try one last idea."

Typing out my text, I hit send before telling myself to reconsider.

He's a friend.

He's come to my aid before.

Maybe he'll do it again.

Who cares that I'll see him all wet and probably looking sexier than hell.

It's a sacrifice I think I'm willing to make.

For the kids...

ME

Hey! What are you doing right now? Oooor say...ten minutes from now? *crosses her fingers and prays like crazy you're free*

HAWKEN

😄 Uh oh. Should I be scared? Who's asking? Is this another one of Dex's schemes to get me to drive somewhere in my underwear?

ME

blinks Umm...is that...do you...I feel like there's a lot to unpack there.

HAWKEN

That's what she said 😜

ME

Sticks fingers in ears NOT LISTENING! NOT LISTENING! Okay maybe I rescind my first question.

HAWKEN

LOL I'm just kidding with you Ror. What's up?

ME

Tatum is sick and Dex is with Summer so he forgot about the dunk tank at my school's carnival that opens in like…eight minutes! I don't mean to sound like a beggar but if you would by ANY chance be free and willing, I promise I'll owe you! I'll do anything at this point!

HAWKEN

Whoa. Careful what you offer, there, Ror. Anything could literally mean…anything,

ME

I know. 😉 But I'm kinda desperate and it's for the kids so it's a sacrifice I guess I'm willing to make.

HAWKEN

No sacrifice needed. How about you feed me after? Fair trade?

ME

OMG YES! I would totally cook for you! That's a great trade!

HAWKEN

Great! I'm already on my way. Be there in five.

ME

You are a lifesaver! 😇 THANK YOU!

HAWKEN

My pleasure. See you soon. 🩶

"Oh shit, I probably shouldn't have sent that."

"Sent what? Who are you talking to?"

I glance at Carissa who has been watching me for the last couple minutes.

"Hawken. He's on his way. He said he'll take over for Dex."

"Perfect!" She smiles. "Then why do you look like you've just been sent to the Principal's office?"

"Uh, no reason?"

She laughs. "That's cute Rory. Fess up girl."

"Ugh. I sent a kiss emoji with that last text."

Her eyes widen. "Rory Foster, are you guys a—"

"No."

Her eyes narrow as she tries to read my now blank expression.

"Buuuuut doooo youuu want to—"

"No." I shake my head.

"Then what are you worried about?"

"I don't know." I tell her with a shrug. "I just don't want to give him the wrong idea I guess."

"Why would he get the wrong idea? It was a straight-forward text."

I chew the inside of my mouth trying to decide if I should tell her all the things or none of the things. "Okay I need to tell you something even though it meant absolutely nothing whatsoever, but I've been dying to tell someone and I can't tell Tatum because she'll tell Dex and then all hell will break loose!"

Carissa jumps up and down clapping her hands. "Ooooh I love stories that start like this. Do tell! Do tell!"

"So, I stopped over at Hawk's the other night. On my way home from a terrible, no good, very bad date."

"Aww, I'm sorry, Ror."

"Yeah, he was a real douche canoe, but that's a story for another day. Anyway, I get to Hawk's and knock on his door and I'm crying because you know, bad night..."

"Yeah."

"And he totally brought me in, gave me a hug, listened to all the things I had to say, and he even made me chocolate milk and he's not the biggest chocolate fan!"

"What?" She frowns. "How does someone not like chocolate?"

"I know, right? Maybe it's a Canada thing? I don't know, but he said he keeps chocolate syrup stocked in his fridge for me because he knows chocolate milk is my favorite."

"Oh my God, Rory! That's so sweet of him." She nudges me. "Sooo...you are interested then?"

"I don't know." My shoulders slump. "My dating record is not good right now and Hawk is Dex's best friend. I can't even imagine how that would go. Especially if it didn't work out, you know? Plus, I really want someone who loves me for me and not who my brother is." I wave away the thought. "Anyway, that's not even the best part."

"Then keep going!" She smiles.

"So, we decide to watch some TV and while he's

making me more chocolate milk, I grab the remote to turn on the television and BAM...PORN!"

Her brows shoot up. "Wait, what?"

I laugh at her shock. "He had been watching porn before I got there. Ooor at some point because there it was. Some woman getting railed by two guys!"

Carissa brings her hand to the base of her neck. "Oh Lord, that's kind of hot. Tell me you watched it together."

"Not a chance. He wanted nothing of it but the whole ordeal was hilarious because he tried to turn it off but ended up pushing the button for another porn channel. It was amazing and suddenly I was seeing Hawken in a whole new light. Okay, maybe not a whole new light. I mean the guy is sex on legs if I'm being honest but yowza!"

"So, what did you end up doing then? You already said you didn't kiss." She gasps. "OH MY GOD! Did you guys fuck?"

I nearly choke on my laugh. "No! We absolutely did not fuck."

"Dammit." She laughs. "I thought this was going to be juicy."

"Sorry to disappoint, but ugh, now I can't stop thinking about Hawk and you know...stuff."

"Giiiiirl, you're crushing on Hawken Malone."

I bring a palm to my forehead. "God, Carissa. What if I am? I cannot be thinking of him like that. I see him around way too often. He's often attached to Dex's hip."

She shrugs with a grin "Maybe it's just an itch..."

"Yeah, maybe."

"Want my advice?"

"Uh, yeah. What would you do?"

"Oh, I would totally scratch that itch."

My eyes nearly pop out of their sockets. "What?" That was not at all what I expected her to say.

"Yep. I'd scratch the itch with every nail I have. Even if it was just one really goooood scratch. Know what I'm sayin'?"

I nod. "Yeah. I hear you."

"Speak of the Devil." She lifts her chin and gestures to the man jogging toward us from the parking lot, his shoulder length dirty blond hair pulled up into one of his signature man-buns behind his Red Tails ballcap. He's dressed in black joggers that button down the sides and hides his solidly fit body under one of the team's many logoed t-shirts. He comes carrying a towel and a pair of flip-flops and when he finally reaches where Carissa and I are standing, his hazel-colored eyes that remind me of the perfect autumn day meet mine.

"Ladies." He greets us with a smile and it's right now I notice the crooked line of his nose, the result of many rough games on the ice, and the sharp square of his jawline. All the guys have rough looking beards now because it's playoff season and nobody shaves. Sometimes I think there's way too much superstition among the team, but they're in the lead right now so who am I to say they're full of hippy dippy bologna?

"Hey Hawken." Carissa gives him a fist bump. "Quick pic, okay? You and Ror?" She smiles at me and I know damn well what she's doing as Hawken reaches around me, swiftly pulling me against him for a picture.

"Thanks."

"No problem." Hawken smiles and then looks down at me. "Where do you want me?"

Underneath me?

Hovering over me?

Between my legs is fine.

I clear my throat. "Uh, I'll show you to the dunk tank. You're here just in time."

"I'll catch up again later, guys." Carissa waves as she heads back toward Colby and Zeke.

"Thank you again for doing this, Hawk. I really, really, REALLY, appreciate it."

"Say no more. It's for the kids and all." He winks. "And I had no plans this evening other than going over a few plays, so you got me out of the house. I should probably be thanking you."

"I was just going to whip up some homemade pizza tonight if you want some. There will be more than enough to share. If you're super nice, I might just be willing to make you your own."

He laughs. "I will never say no to pizza. That sounds great. Thanks."

"Alright, well, this is the dunk tank, so you'll enter through this little gate here and have a seat on the platform. When the kids throw the ball and hit the target, in you go. Simple as that."

"Sounds good." He sets his towel and flip flops on the mat behind the dunk tank. "Did you make sure the water was a balmy eighty-five degrees for me?"

"Ha! In your dreams, buddy."

He throws his head back in laughter. "Worth a shot, eh?"

"Just keep reminding yourself it's for the kids, Malone. You can shower at my place afterwards and make the water as hot as you want."

"Right." He winks. "For the kids. Got it."

Dear Jesus, why is he so...itchy?

Once Hawken is squared away, I do a quick check to make sure everyone is in their stations and then I give permission for the PTO President to open the gate.

"Let the carnival begin!"

5

HAWKEN

"**Y**ou think that was a shot? My blind grandmother could've made a better shot than that!"

Confession time. My initial intention in coming here tonight was not for the kids. It was one thousand percent for Rory because I know how much this event means to her and the school. But now that I'm here and have yet to be dunked, I'm quite enjoying razzing the kids as they give it their best try.

"Oh yeah?" The little boy twists his mouth trying not to smile. "Well...umm...you only wish you were as good as Milo Landric! He's the best guy on our whole team!"

Whoa!

The kid's got balls!

I throw my head back in laughter. "You know what? You got me there, son. I do wish I were half as good as Landric is. What's your name kid?"

"Micah."

"Micah, what grade are you in?"

"Fifth."

"Micah, do you think you're ever going to be able to hit this target?"

The kid smirks. "Yeah."

"I mean, really?" I cock my head and raise a brow, egging him on. "Because let's be honest here, you've missed the first two so what do I need to do to sweeten the pot?"

His hands go to his hips as his friends all whisper in his ear. "What are you offering, old man?"

Old man.

Raises fist at the young whippersnapper

Whyyy I oughta...

"You've got two more shots, right?"

"Yep."

"How about you get me with this next hit and I'll give you a signed puck?"

His eyes light up. "From Landric? A signed puck from Landric?"

This kid.

I like him.

He's a cute little shit with balls bigger than mine.

"Well that all depends." I laugh. "You gonna keep your eye on the target this time or not?"

Micah laughs with a shake of his head, but I can see he's accepting the challenge. The gauntlet has been thrown and he's picked it up. He gets himself into focus mode, rubbing the ball between his hands, and then he pitches it as hard as he can.

And misses.

I throw my arms up. "See, the problem here is that you asked for Landric's autograph but that big man isn't even here today, Micah!" I pat my chest. "You've got me. The one and only Hawken Malone and I'm about to sweeten the pot even more because I like you, kid."

He laughs again and I'm really glad he's taking my teasing in stride.

"This is your last try so let's make it worth it, eh?"

"Yeah!"

"You get me in this water and I've got an entire suite at the arena for you and your whole class. How's that sound?"

All the kids standing around who overhear our conversation are now gathered around watching.

"You're on!" Micah shouts as his friends all cheer him on, clapping him on the shoulder and patting his back in encouragement. He'll most likely miss but I'll give him the tickets anyway because no way in hell am I rescinding an offer to a kid no matter what the reasoning, but it's nice to see all the kids coming together to support their friend and classmate.

"Hey, Malone!"

I turn my head just in time to see Rory walking over to Micah and his friends, the sway to her hips a movement I am certain to catch. "You razzing on my buddy Micah over here?"

"Heck yeah, I am. Offered him a signed puck and he still missed!"

"I was just holding out for more, Ms. Foster. Like you said."

"Like she...WHAT?" The smile and shock that spreads across my face when she winks at me says it all.

She totally played me.

And I fell for it.

"Ms. Foster did you set me up?"

She grins back at me like the fucking Christmas Grinch with a bag full of Whoville decorations and passes me a playful shrug.

"I don't know what you're talking about, Malone." She looks back to Micah. "Did he offer tickets?"

He nods. "Sure did! A suite for the whole class!"

She offers Micah a fist bump and then gestures toward me. "Show him what you're really made of kid."

The kid barely even fucking blinks before he winds up and pitches the ball my way with all his might and I'm a wet mess for the first time today. When I resurface, I shake the water from my head and clear my eyes just in time to see Rory pass by with a wicked wink.

"Well played, Foster, well played. You're lucky I can't pull you in here with me. I'd have you drenched in no time."

She snickers. "In your dreams, Malone." But I swear to God when she walks away, I hear her say "And mine."

"Thank you again for jumping in last minute today. I think the kids loved you." I follow Rory into the elevator and up to the penthouse she used to share with her brother. I've spent more hours in this place than I should probably admit but never have I been here without Dex. It's weird, but it doesn't necessarily feel wrong either...which is also weird.

"My pleasure. I was happy to do it. Plus, it got me out

of the house for the evening so I don't feel like an unsocial-ized sad sap."

She frowns as she opens the door. "Umm, I hardly think you're a sad sap, Hawken. Why would you say that?"

"Because up until, well, now I guess, my social time has always included your brother in one way or another. But he was nowhere to be seen today."

"Which reminds me, I should text him and make sure Tate's okay," she murmurs, tossing her keys on the hook by the door.

"Already done. Tate's still feeling a little nauseous but her nap helped with the headache. Also, I told him his lack of attendance cost me a suite full of fifth graders."

"Oh, I bet he had a field day with that one."

"He definitely found it funny. Told me he was proud of you though for pulling one over on me."

She giggles. "I learned from the best you know."

"Obviously."

Rory heads straight to the kitchen and pulls out all the ingredients to make pizzas. "I have dough from Maximo's around the corner. I hope that's okay with you."

"Yeah, perfect. How did I not know you could get dough there?"

She smirks. "Because you can't."

"Oh."

She stops momentarily and leans her hip against the counter. "Okay so this might be one of the only times I've ever used my relation to Dex to my advantage."

"Oh really? For pizza dough? That's the hill you're prepared to die on?"

"Uh, yeah. Have you even had Maximo's before?"

"Sweetheart if they're right around the corner from you, they're right around the corner from me, so that would be a resounding yes. Plus, his salads are tasty too. The house dressing?" I kiss my fingertips. "Mmm! Chef's kiss."

"Agreed!"

"So, tell me how you're gettin' the dough."

She smiles and raises her shoulder. "I couldn't stop raving about it when Dex and I were in there one day a few years ago. And then I posted about it on social media but I used Dex's account because you know...celebrity status and all."

"Right."

"So, the next time we were in there Maximo himself came out to thank Dex for the amazing shout-out because his business had picked up since that post, especially with out of towners who were in for a game."

"No shit!"

"Right? It's true though. He told Dex if there was ever anything he could do, he'd make it happen. So Dex told him I love to experiment with pizzas at home and asked if he could take a couple balls of dough home. Maximo said anytime he wants it to come get it."

"How did I never know this?"

"It's not something we tell people. Well, Dex didn't want me to blab to the world that we're getting free pizza dough whenever we want it. Plus, we basically pay for it every time we go in because Dex is a ridiculously generous tipper. I'm not even sure he's ever looked at the bill before. He just drops a few hundred-dollar bills on the table and walks." She shakes her head. "You boys and your piles of cash."

"Hey at least he's using it for good."

"Oh yeah, I'll never complain about the way he spends his money. It's his. God knows he's worked his ass off for it and he's always treated people well. If his head ever starts to get too big, I'm always there to remind him of the kind of paychecks we normal people make. He appreciates the reminder sometimes."

"So, what do you like on your pizza?" I ask her. "Are you one of those pineapple on or pineapple off?"

"Mmmm a Hawaiian chicken pizza is incredible! I'm team pineapple, but oh my God, don't come near me with an anchovy."

"Girl after my own heart. On that we can definitely agree."

"What about you? Like anything special?" She digs through her toppings. "I've got pepperoni, green peppers, banana peppers, onions, tomatoes, black olives, mushrooms, bacon pieces..."

"Wow that's a lot of toppings for one little person." Good Lord, there's no way she eats that much.

"Well, I'm always prepared for Dex and Tatum to be around. Plus, I'll use these in other dishes too."

"Right. That makes sense. Umm, You know what? I like all those toppings so why don't you surprise me while I grab a shower if you don't mind?"

"Oh yeah. Totally! You can use the guest bathroom if you want but the ensuite bathroom off my room is the best one. Fantastic water pressure. Walk in ready. Towels are on the shelf just inside."

"Thanks."

"Sure. I'll get these made up and pop them in the oven. Ready in about twenty minutes."

"Perfect. I'm famished."

I make my way down the familiar hallway to where I know Dex's room used to be but now belongs to Rory. A contended smile spreads across my face at the style of this room that is so clearly her eclectic personality. An explosion of colorful decor surrounds a large bed covered in fluffy white linens. A dark navy blue velvet upholstered headboard is an eye-catchingly beautiful choice for a statement piece.

Hanging around the space are collections of...hmm, how do I describe this...unique pieces of art. On one wall, a pair of hands clasped together, painted legs in the air, the silhouette of a naked female, and one framed quote that reads *You are enough just as you are.* On the opposite wall is a collection of baby animals. A duckling, a kitten, a puppy, and a squirrel playing together with another framed quote that says *Everyone deserves someone who makes them look forward to tomorrow.* She has a long mirror standing along the front wall next to a dresser, the words *You are stunning as fuck!* written in black sharpie along the top in what I don't believe to be her handwriting. I've seen it enough times to know this wasn't written by her and now I can't fight the stab of jealousy that overcomes me at the thought of another man possibly writing it for her.

She doesn't bring other guys here.

Does she?

Based on our conversation a few nights ago, I would say no.

But I could be wrong, I guess.

In the corner of the room sits a slightly oversized yellow armchair that looks both like something purchased at a flea market but also something I can see Rory relaxing in with a blanket and her favorite book. My eyes fall to the red throw blanket strewn across the chair, the edge of a white box peeking out from underneath. Curious, I lift the blanket to get a better look at the box and find it to be clear of any logo or design stating what might be inside. Because I'm a bit of an impertinent asshole who needs to know what's in the box, I lift the lid to peek inside and holy shit. I did not expect this.

Rory's a woman. I get it.

An attractive woman with needs and desires just like anyone else, so of course she has toys. In fact, if I recall correctly, she joked about having several not too long ago. Can't judge her for that, but holy fucking shit, I never expected she would own one that has my name on it.

The Hawk.

It's not on a product label, but it is her handwriting on the inside lid of the box.

The Hawk.

She named her vibrator The Hawk?

Did *she* name it?

Or was this the product's name and she wrote it down to keep track?

I shake my head. "There's no way this is a coincidence," I mumble, thinking back to a particular Christmas gift she gave me years ago.

"Hey man! What are you doing here? Shouldn't you be on a plane home for Christmas?" Dex holds the door open and I step inside. Rory is wrapped up on the couch in a

fuzzy blanket. Her black hair pulled up in a messy knot on the top of her head. She's adorably dressed in her holiday footie pj's that I've seen a few times now. For a split second I feel bad that I'm intruding on their movie watching but I really wanted to see them before I head out of town.

"Yeah," I nod. "I have to be at the airport in a little over an hour, but I wanted to make sure I delivered your presents before I left town. I'm sorry I won't be here to celebrate with you two."

"What?" Dex's brow furrows. "Dude, you never have to bring presents here. You know that." His frown turns into a smirk. "But I'm glad you stopped by because it just so happens, I do have something for you."

"See asshole?" I laugh. "If I would've come here empty handed, I would've felt like a shmuck. Hey, Rory."

"Hi Hawken," she says with a wave and a smile. "Merry Christmas."

"Merry Christmas to you too. Watching Elf *again*, eh?"

"Don't judge me," she giggles. "It's Christmas break and I'm indulging in my inner child."

I shake my head with a soft laugh. "No judgement here. You look adorable as always." Lifting a package from my arms I hand it to her. "I got you something."

Her brows shoot up in surprise. "Wait, me? You got me something?"

"Yeah. I did."

"Why?"

"Uh, because I wanted to?"

She springs up from the couch, her blanket landing on the floor. "Wait! I got you something too! Well, a few some-things, actually."

I watch her practically skip over to their brightly decorated Christmas tree and grab one of the stockings lying underneath the tree. "Merry Christmas, Hawk."

My eyes widen and my mouth falls open. "You seriously did this? For me?"

"Yeah." She smiles. "I make a stocking for Dex every year so, you know, I figured I would do one for you too. You practically live here too, you know."

"Rory." I shake my head in disbelief. "This is one of the nicest things anyone has ever done for me. Thank you."

"Well don't say that, yet, silly. You might hate everything inside. Go on. Open it."

I pull out the gifts one at a time, excited about each one. Deodorizers for my equipment bag, a bag of my favorite lemon sour candies, a new charm for my Crocs, and my favorite gift, a new water bottle specifically engraved for me. When I unwrap it and turn it in my hand, I laugh at the name scrolled on the side.

"The Hawk." I shake my head with a laugh. "This is perfect, Rory. I love it."

"It promises to keep hot things hot and cold things cold so..." She shrugs. "You know."

"And locks so it doesn't leak. Perfect for my flight today. Thank you, Rory."

"You're welcome. Merry Christmas Hawken."

The Hawk.

She's named one of her sex toys The Hawk.

This is both unbelievable and the most amazing thing I think I've ever witnessed. The toy inside is rather large for someone like Rory. Girthy, and with a little weight to it as I pick it up and hold it. The dark purple silicone is smooth in my hand and although it feels nice, there's no way she's getting the true feeling of a veiny ribbed dick with this thing.

Still, turning it around in my hand it appears as though it both fucks and sucks at the same time and now there's a visual in my mind that will live rent free for eternity.

Fuck me, she's had this thing inside her.

Why do I suddenly want to taste it to see if I can taste her?

Don't be stupid Hawken.

Put it away.

The last thing I need is for her to walk in here and catch me holding her dildo in my hand. No amount of explaining will save me if that happens. I place it gently back in its box and slide the box under the red blanket. Before I get anymore entranced with the wonderland that is Rory's bedroom, which smells heavenly, like coconut and the beach, I turn into the bathroom and grab a towel from the shelf, closing the door behind me.

Pulling off my swim trunks and t-shirt from the dunk tank, I step inside the marbled shower and let the hot water run over my body. The pressure juts against my back, giving my muscles some much needed relief.

My mind, on the other hand, is now reeling with thoughts of Rory.

Jesus Christ, she fucks herself with that thing.

The Hawk.

I can't get the visual out of my head now. Of her relaxed against that yellow chair. Her legs wide open and resting on the arms. Her hands guiding The Hawk inside her, twisting, turning, circling along the innermost sensitive parts of her sweet, dripping pussy.

Fuck...me.

Does she whisper my name as she touches herself?

"Hawken..."

Does she scream my name when she comes?

"Oh God! Hawken!"

Does she think of me?

Am I getting this all wrong?

I don't know but before I can even consider stopping myself, my stiffened cock is in my hands and I'm pumping away to thoughts of watching my best friend's sister get herself off with a toy she named after me.

I'm totally about to jack off in Rory's shower.

I know I shouldn't.

But I can't stop myself.

I don't want to stop myself.

"Jesus, fuck," I murmur as I pull at my shaft, my balls beginning to tighten as I squeeze the base and rub my hand up and down.

Up and down.

Up and down.

Faster and faster, squeezing tighter and thrusting myself through my fist imagining myself fucking Rory, hearing her call out to me, until my mouth hangs open and I'm coming so fucking hard in Rory's shower I almost black out.

God that was...

I'm breathless.

That was amazing.

But also, I am sooo going straight to hell.

I give myself a moment to recover and then quickly soap up and rinse before turning off the water and grabbing my towel. Pulling my clean clothes out of my duffle bag, I slip into a pair of black trainers, sans t-shirt for now, while I continue to dry off. Then throw my dirty clothes into my bag and then step back into Rory's room.

I stop in front of her yellow chair, thinking once again about what I know to be inside the white box peeking out from under the blanket.

Rory Foster never ceases to amaze me.

These last few years that I've known her, she's been the supportive younger sister of a hockey star and compassionate teacher of tiny humans. She's been a woman with a fun personality who knows how to take a joke, especially when it comes from the guys on the team, but she also takes no shit from anyone...well, except for the douche bags she's dated. Why she's taken their bullshit repeatedly I'll never know because she's better than that. She's someone I've developed a deep respect for, and I find myself wanting to know her on an entirely different level.

A more personal level.

An intimate one.

I don't exactly know where these feelings are coming from. Maybe I'm lonelier than I thought. Or maybe watching my friends and teammates settle down and find love is making me rethink my life and what I want for myself. Either way, Rory Foster is on my mind often these days. I like how she makes me feel when she's around. She makes me smile. She makes me laugh. The more I'm around her, the more time I spend with her, the more I crave her. If she would give me the chance, I could show her I wouldn't be one of those guys who only wants her because of who her brother is. I can be a friend to Dex and more than a friend to Rory too.

At this point, I know her better than any other guy does.

Even more than her brother.

I could be the kind of man she's looking for.

I could take care of her.

I could do a better job satisfying her than any damn toy she could possibly own.

I really think I want that with her.

Which is why I'm not stopping myself from lifting the lid one last time and pulling The Hawk from its white box. I drop the box onto the floor pushing it just underneath the chair and then lay The Hawk on top of the red blanket out in the open. This way she'll know I saw it. That I had my hands on it. That I put it here.

And then I'll wait.

I can be patient with Rory.

She needs that.

And for as much as I want her, maybe I need it too, because navigating these waters without Dex finding out until I figure out how to handle things with him could be tricky as fuck.

6

RORY

I hear Hawken pad down the hallway just as the timer goes off.

"Perfect timing," I call out as I open the oven and pull out two perfectly baked round pizzas. "How was your —hoooooly..." My eyes catch sight of the tightly sculpted abdomen of Hawken Malone, each muscle perfectly rippled and leading to the magnificent V that I only ever get to read about in my dirty romance books. The one I know leads to the most glorious piece of him I will only ever get to dream about.

And maybe jill off to when I'm alone at night.

Because let's be honest, he's my brother's best friend.

That's a line I'm not sure I could get myself to cross no matter how sexy the man is.

Except oooh God, Hawken Malone could be such a treat...

Just envisioning him dripping wet and stepping out of my shower completely naked, palming his hardened—

"What's that?" he asks after he drops his duffle bag by

the front door and saunters toward the kitchen. His shoulder-length hair is still wet as he reaches back and pulls it into a bun. His t-shirt hanging over his shoulder, he grabs it and stretches it over his head pulling it down over him.

Noooooooo!

I don't want to wake up from this dream!

Five more minutes!

"Oh, um..." I clear my throat and come back to reality. "How was the shower?"

"Amazing." He smiles at me. "The pressure in there... you were right."

"Told ya. I'm glad you feel better. And dinner is ready. I made one with all veggies and one with meats. I'm sorry it might be a bit boring this time, but I know you try to keep to a diet. Especially with the playoffs. I don't want to be the reason *the* Hawken Malone has a bad game so I'm keeping it simple for tonight."

He bows his head almost bashfully and then meets my gaze with a heated stare. "Rory you will never be the reason I have a bad game so cut that shit out right now. This looks and smells amazing. But also, if this is simple," he says gesturing to the food in front of us, "then call me intrigued. I want to be around to sample more of what you have to offer."

Good God, if ever there were a time when I nearly choke on a man's words, it's right now. As it is, I have to turn around so he doesn't see me blush. I open another cupboard and grab a couple plates, giving my face the chance to fix itself before turning back around.

"When the season is over, it's a deal. We can play around and experiment all you want."

Jesus, Rory.

Don't egg him on.

I cut us each a couple slices from each pizza and hand him a plate and then take the seat next to him at the island bar. He takes his first bite and I watch with joy as his eyes roll back and he moans with pleasure. "Mmm fuck, this might be the most amazing pizza I've ever had."

I give him a teasing slap to the bicep. "Stop it. Don't tease me."

"I'm not teasing, Ror." He shakes his head and takes another huge bite. "This is fucking delicious. Not too heavy on the sauce. I can literally taste every ingredient. Right down to the...is that basil and sea salt?"

My jaw practically drops. "Uh, yeah. How did you know that?"

His eyes bulge but he talks with his mouth full and a goofy smile on his face. "Because it's fucking good, Foster. Seriously. I think you may have missed your calling with this whole teaching thing. You need your own restaurant."

"Whoa, let's not get too ahead of ourselves there, Malone." The idea of me as a restaurant owner makes me laugh. "I like my littles. They're crazy tiny humans and I get the extreme pleasure of introducing them to the world of creativity and imagination. Plus, I wouldn't want to have to deal with angry, meticulous customers."

"I guess that makes sense. Maybe I can just hire you to be my own personal chef."

"HA! You can't afford me."

"Oh, no?"

"Nope." I shake my head adamantly.

"You know I make millions right? Quite sure I could afford you."

"You know I cost multi-millions right? Sooo quite sure you can't afford me. Now, maybe if you were someone more like, I don't know, Milo Landric."

A belly laugh escapes him when I pass him a wink and a teasing shrug. "Fucking Milo. God, that kid really had me going today. Landric was probably in on it."

"Now that would've been funny." I nod excitedly, wiping my mouth with my napkin. "I should've thought of that."

"You thought of enough. I fell for your shenanigans hook, line, and sinker."

"You definitely sunk, that's for sure."

"Yeah, you're welcome, by the way."

I grasp his forearm tenderly. "Thank you, Hawken. I really do sincerely appreciate you stepping in on a moment's notice for me. Err...for the kids I mean."

"You know I like helping when kids are involved, but if I'm being honest, I didn't do it for them. I did it for you."

I don't quite know what to say to that.

Hawken has always been cordial to me when he's been here hanging out with Dex in past years. He's never been disrespectful. In fact, maybe it's because he knows Dex so well that he's been such a comfort for me when I've needed it.

His friendship never wavers.

Besides Dex, I feel closer and more comfortable around Hawken than anyone else on the team, but sometimes, like right now, I almost wish he were more of a dick. At least that way it would be easier to control my thoughts and feelings around him. Since Dex and Tatum have moved out, I've started to see Hawken in a whole new light.

A light that makes me smile when I think about it.

A light that makes me hot and bothered when I'm alone.

A light that makes me wonder what life could be like if we were...more.

And that scares me a little because if we started something and it were to go sour, it could be detrimental for Hawken and my brother. Not that I should care what my brother thinks about my relationships. I don't care. He doesn't control me. But I know how hard he's worked to find the success he has now. I know how much he cares for Hawken. They've been inseparable for years. If I were to come between that...

Okay. Okay.

Enough of this thinking.

Stop going there.

Shaking my thoughts from my head, I pass Hawken a smile and reiterate how much I appreciate him. And then I stuff another bite of pizza into my mouth.

We both eat a couple more slices and then Hawken wipes his mouth with his napkin, watching me.

"What?"

He smiles. "Tell me something about you I don't know."

I catch myself from laughing. "Uh, like what?"

"I don't know." He shakes his head. "There must be something. Any hidden talents I don't know about?"

I cock my head. "You say that like you actually know of hidden talents I already have."

"I do."

"Like what?"

"I know you make some of the best pizza I've ever had."

Okay now I snort. "That hardly counts."

"Sure, it does. You're clearly magical. What else can you do?"

"Umm, okay let's see. I can solve a Rubik's Cube in under thirty seconds."

His brows peak. "Seriously?"

"Mhmm."

"Show me. Do you have one around here?"

"Yeah. Over there on that bookshelf." I point across the room to one of the white bookshelves against the wall. Hawken steps over and grabs the Rubik's Cube, holding it up for me to see.

"May I?"

I nod. "Please. All you want."

He narrows his eyes at me. "Don't watch. That's cheating."

"Okay. You mess it up while I clear our plates."

I throw our paper plates in the garbage and store the left-over pizza in a few containers inside the fridge before joining Hawken in the living room.

"Thirty seconds? You're serious?"

"Yeah. No problem."

"I don't see how it's possible."

"Neither does Dex. He thinks I'm some sort of possessed demon every time I do it."

"Alright, let's see then."

Plopping down next to him on the couch, he places the

cube in my hand. I turn it over a few times, getting a good look at the tile placement.

"Ready?" he asks, pulling his phone from his pocket and setting the timer.

"Yep. Ready."

"Okay, go."

Once I begin, muscle memory takes over and I'm flipping the layers between my hands in the exact order I've always learned, completing the white side first, and then the others one color at a time until they're all locked in place. In less than the allotted time, I toss Hawken my finished cube and he is dumbfounded.

"Holy shit, you really did it." His jaw drops. "How the fuck did you do that?"

I shrug innocently. "Magic."

He laughs. "No shit. That's seriously impressive. Tell me something else."

"*If-a I-a oldta ouya orema Ia ouldwa alfha ota illka ouya.*"

"Right. Fuck." He snorts, wiping his hand down his face. "I forgot you speak fluent pig Latin. God, I used to hate when Dex would do that."

"Yeah, well, we communicated daily that way when we were young. Our parents..." I roll my eyes. "Or lack thereof. You know."

"Yeah." He nods. "Dex has talked about it. I'm sure it was rough."

"It could've been a lot worse for us, clearly. I'm really proud of Dex for keeping himself on track and focused on his dream. And I'm grateful he kind of took me along with him. He didn't have to do that."

"Your brother is a good guy, Ror. He loves you a lot."

"I know he does. The feeling is mutual." I turn to him with a pointed finger. "But if you ever tell him I said that, I'll never speak to you again."

He raises his hands in defense. "Your secret is safe with me."

"Sooo what about you?" I nudge him with my shoulder. "Do you have a hidden talent?"

"I can shoot a rubber disk into a net at a pretty fuckin' fast speed."

"Nope." I shake my head with a laugh. "Doesn't count. You get paid to do that."

"Oh, so that's not a talent?"

"Not a talent. That's a trained skill. Plus, it's too obvious and I already know about that so dig deeper Malone."

"Okay, okay. Umm." He snaps his fingers. "I'm pretty damn good at D.D.R."

"Correction." I smile. "You're good enough to beat the rest of the guys during video game night but you've never beat me so you're not that good. And again, I've seen you do it many times so Dance Dance Revolution doesn't count either."

"Son of a bitch," he huffs playfully. "Alright. I've got one more."

"Okay, let's hear it."

"What if I told you I could swing dance?"

My eyes grow huge and I inhale a deep gasp. "Shut. Up! Can you?"

"Yeah." He shakes his head. "I don't know why, but it

became this...thing back in high school. There was a swing club and everything."

"Canadians swing dance?" I squeal. "This is amazing! You have to show me!"

"And how do you propose I do that?"

"Dance with me!" I spring up from the couch. "I danced for years growing up. Dex had hockey, I had dance!" I spin around until I spot my wireless. "Oh, my God, Hawk! I had no idea you knew how to dance for real! Had I known I might have dragged you out with me ages ago!"

"Can you even imagine what the paparazzi would do with videos of me swing dancing?" He chuckles. "I don't know how much I'll remember. It's been a while."

"Bullshit." I laugh, offering him my hand and pulling him off the couch with me, then pushing the coffee table out of the way so we have an open floor. "It's muscle memory. Your body will just do it." I pick up my phone and scroll through my dance playlists. "'Zoot Suit Riot' okay?"

"Uh, sure."

"Eeek! Okay, here we go!" I link my speaker to my Bluetooth and then hit play in my music app, tossing my phone to the couch. Neither one of us are dressed for swing dancing but hell if this isn't the coolest thing to learn about Hawken Malone. As soon as the music starts to play, a smile erupts across my face.

It's been too long since I've let myself enjoy a moment of dance. As the beat of the drum set starts us off, we both shake out our arms and hands preparing for what's to come. When I glance at Hawken, he smiles back at me just as the band starts to wail and away we go. He grabs my hand and twists his arm around my waist, leading me around the floor as our feet move to the upbeat sound of one of my favorite swing songs. His arm falls away as I flip and turn but then his hand is right there to pull me back in toward his body all over again. His strength when he holds me, his confidence guiding me across the floor, it's sexy as hell. This so much fucking fun! I can't believe I didn't know this about him before.

Where has this been all my life?

Our hands stay connected as we kick our feet and twist our hips laughing through the fun and after a minute or so, with a mischievous wink, he turns this dance up a notch.

"You ready?"

"Ready?"

"Let's see if you can keep up, Lady Bug."

"Lady Bug?"

He's never called me that before.

"Well, I almost said jitterbug, but you deserve a prettier nickname than that."

When the band kicks back in, his energy starts to build and then he's lifting me and flipping me over his shoulder and then pulling me through his legs. With his strength, he can practically throw me across the floor but I land on two feet and keep right on dancing with more happiness in my soul than I have felt in an exceptionally long time.

With the rattle of the saxophone, Hawken slaps his legs and pulses to the beat as I twirl and turn toward him and then he grabs my hand and we continue the give and take of this dance. Before the song ends, he lifts me once again, bringing me to one side of him and then another, flipping me in his arms and cradling my head in his hand before he pulls me back up against him, his arm wrapped around my waist.

Both of us panting as we try to catch our breath, we stare into each other's eyes and I'm speechless.

I had no idea he had this hidden talent.

"Hawken...that was..." I shake my head, breathless. "Amazing!"

"Yeah...it was." His smile falters and the look in his eye as he stares at me makes me wonder what he could possibly be thinking about.

Did he not enjoy himself?

Was I not good enough?

I know it's been a while but...

"Hawk? You okay? Did I—"

He pushes his strong hand through my hair and pulls my face toward his, silencing me when his lips come down over mine. He's not gentle but he's not forceful by any means. He's soft but eager, and when his tongue slides over the seam of my lips they part for him without question, allowing him the opportunity to take what he wants like I've wanted this from him all along. He sweeps his tongue inside my mouth, tasting me, filling me, and I find myself sinking into the feel of him, not wanting him to ever leave.

He should add kissing to his list of hidden talents.

A small whimper escapes me when his other arm slides around my waist, his fingers dancing across my bare skin peeking out where my shirt went askew from dancing. His touch is warm and it sends a slamming pulse to parts of me that have been dormant for way too long and now I wish his fingers would go—

No.

This can't happen.

It shouldn't happen.

Fuck, if it were any other teammate.

But it isn't.

It's Hawken.

He's Dex's best friend.

He's basically forbidden.

As quickly as he started it, I end it, pushing away from him, breathless and a little shocked at what I just allowed to happen.

"Hawken, I—"

"I'm sorry," his response is fast. He shakes his head slowly. "I shouldn't have...I didn't mean t—"

"No, it's fine. I—"

"I mean I did, I just—"

"We probably shou—"

"Yeah. You're right, but I—"

"Maybe we should ju—"

"I should...go." He hitches his thumb back behind him toward the door as he begins to back away from me. "Big day tomorrow, you know, with the...game."

"Yeah."

Shit. Why do I feel like I'm messing this up when I don't even know what this is to begin with? What just happened and what is happening now? Why does this feel so fucking awkward? And why do I feel like I could cry right now?

"Hawken?"

"Yeah?" He slides into his shoes and hooks his duffle bag onto his shoulder.

"Thanks...for the dance." I say it almost like a question.

"Thanks for dinner." He gives me a quick smile and then he's out the door, leaving me to stand alone in my now very empty penthouse apartment. Usually when weird things like this happen with a guy, I overthink them and end up crying myself to sleep, or as in the case a few nights ago, I cry to Hawken about them. He's been my friend all these years. He's a great comfort for me. But when weird things happen that involve Hawken... what am I supposed to do?

"Dammit."

"That kiss. It was," I bring my fingertips to my lips, "so good." I lean my head back and close my eyes, remembering what his hand felt like on my skin. How he made me smile as we danced, and like magic, that pulse inside me returns.

The hum of desire.

The whisper of lust.

My body knows what it wants.

My body will take me right where I need to be.

To my bedroom.

For a visit with my very favorite toy. The one I very appropriately nicknamed The Hawk because I've used it more times than I care to admit getting myself off to thoughts of Hawken Malone.

Locking the door, I shut off the lights as I head toward my bedroom and over to my chair but the moment I get there I stop short.

Something's different.

The Hawk.

It's not in its box.

Quickly glancing around the room, I gasp. "Fuck! Did he see this?"

I pick up my favorite dildo perfect in girth and length, examining it and looking for its box, which I find under the chair. I flip open the lid wondering if I'll find some sort of note. A "Gotcha" prank I might be falling for, but there's nothing here.

Did I leave this here?

Is this my fault?

No way.

I never leave it out.

I know it was under my red blanket.

That can only mean one thing.

Hawken had to have seen it.

Hawken Malone met The Hawk.

And I don't know now if I'll live to tell the tale.

7
HAWKEN

I haven't seen or heard from Rory in a week and now I'm paranoid as fuck that she's avoiding me. I'm even more paranoid that she may have told Dex what happened and it's beginning to eat at me more than I thought it would. What excuse would I have for kissing his sister? None. I don't have one except for I wanted to. That entire day spent in Rory's presence made me feel more alive than I've felt in a long time.

Like I meant something.

Like I had a bit of a purpose other than just winning hockey games.

It was nice to be needed.

It was nice to be needed by Rory.

Being in her apartment...her bedroom...her bathroom... seeing the fucking Hawk. And then laughing with her. Dancing with her. Everything about her was catching me by surprise and in that moment when I was holding her in my arms, everything flashed before my eyes. I wanted her. I wanted to claim her. I wanted to taste her. Now I'm craving more. More of her. And I'm not exactly sure what to do about it.

We won the first three games of the second round of playoffs against New York, and tonight we aim to make it a four-game sweep before heading home. I should be a ball of ecstatic energy. I should be pumped as fuck and ready to pull out this next win, and while part of me is all those things, my mind is stuck on Rory Foster, and when I might be able to kiss her again.

Not if.

When.

My legs work of their own accord as I let my arms hang over the handlebars of the exercise bike. Sweat drips down my face. Out of the corner of my eye I spot Dex when he walks into the gym to start his lifts. He doesn't look particularly happy, nor does he have a smart remark to make about taint sweat on the bike seat when he sees me here and that's a huge red flag. Dex is always the one to make off-the-cuff remarks. The ones that have us all rolling our eyes and laughing. But not this time. I'm not sure he's said more than a word to anyone today, least of all me.

Fuck.

Does he know?

Did Rory tell him?

What do I say if she did?

Should I text her and ask?

Should we get our story straight?

"What's the matter with you, man?"

"Huh?" I shake my thoughts from my mind when Quinton sits down on the bike next to me. "What do you mean? I'm fine."

"You don't look fine. You look like the scared teenager who doesn't want to be called on by the teacher."

"That's oddly specific, Quinton."

"I'm just saying you look worried. What are you worried about?"

Swallowing my pride a little, I gesture to where Dex is lifting and murmur to Quinton, "What's going on with him today?"

A smirk crosses his face. "Don't know. Why? Trouble in friendship paradise?"

"Uh, no. Why would you think that? Did he say that?"

"No, but you're giving it away asshat." He chuckles and leans over to speak a little quieter. "You're not very good at this, you know."

"Good at what?"

I'm suddenly spinning faster on this damn bike and the sweat feels like it's rolling off me in waves.

"Good at hiding shit. What did you do?"

"What do you mean what did I do?"

He narrows his eyes. "You did something."

"I didn't do anything."

"Something you don't want him knowing about?"

"What? No." I scoff.

"Mhmm." He smiles. "Tell me more."

"Oh, fuck off, Shay. I didn't do anything to Dex. I was just wondering why he seems like he's in a mood."

He shrugs. "Well if you don't know, I sure as hell don't."

"Know what?" Milo asks, tossing his towel next to his water bottle and stepping up on one of the nearby treadmills.

Quinton gestures to Dex, who thank God, is oblivious to our conversation with his earbuds in, which are probably blaring his workout playlist. "Hawken wants to know why Dex is in a mood?"

"Uh oh." Milo whistles. "What did you do to him, Malone?"

I laugh to mask my guilt. "I swear I did nothing."

"Well, you guys are basically in a bromance so..." Milo shrugs with a smirk. "You should know why he's in a mood, right?"

"For the love of Christ, we are not in a br—

"Who's in a mood?" Zeke asks when he pulls out his earbud after his run ends.

"Dex," Milo tells him.

"Dex is in a mood? What for?"

I shake my head. "No reason."

Quinton's curiosity and penchant for riling up the team gets the better of him. "Because Hawken did something he shouldn't have and now Dex is mad about it."

I roll my eyes. "Jesus Christ, Quinton."

Colby gasps. "The lovers are fighting? What did you do Hawken?"

"Oh my God! Why do you all assume I did something to the guy? I didn't do anything to him, I swear."

"Just come out with it." Colby smiles. "You know you won't be able to keep it a secret for long."

"Yeah, plus if it's something that's going to really piss him off, we should know," Milo adds.

Zeke nods. "Yeah, especially if it's going to affect his game play, you know?"

Colby grows serious. "Is it going to affect his game play? Don't fuck with him, Malone."

Quinton points to Zeke. "Zeke's right. You better just tell us."

"Oh, for fuck's sake." I hang my head and try to weigh my options as quickly as possible.

Tell them or don't tell them?

Can they help me or not?

Fuck.

Here goes nothing.

"I kissed his sister."

Yep. That just spilled right out of my mouth.

And now my jaw is on the floor.

Right next to four other jaws.

At the same time—at least it feels like it happens simultaneously—all four guys look at Dex and then look back at me, eyes wide.

"Oh, my God. Avert your eyes assholes!"

"You did WHAT?" Milo asks with a shocked albeit excited expression on his face.

I bow my head and peer over my shoulder a bit to make sure he's not looking because the fucking cat is out of the bag and there's nobody to blame but me. "I...I kissed her."

"You kissed Rory."

"Yes."

Quinton grins. "Rory Foster."

"Yes."

"When? When did this happen?"

"Last week."

Zeke's eyes bulge. "Not at the school carnival?"

I shake my head. "After."

Colby hands me my water bottle, his face a little more serious. "Did you sleep with her Hawk?"

"What? No! It wasn't like that."

Quinton whistles softly. "You're right to be scared, man. Dex will be livid when he finds out."

"He can't find out." I shake my head adamantly. "It was nothing. Probably won't happen again. He doesn't need to know."

"Probably?" Zeke's brow raises. "Who are you trying to convince, Hawk? Rory or yourself?"

"Fuck. I don't know," I mumble. "Do you think he would really be that pissed?"

Quinton nearly cackles. "Dude! You know his number one rule. He goes over it every fucking year."

"I will rip your balls off, roast them over open coals, and shove them down your throat if you even think about touching my sister."

"Rory Foster is off limits, man. You know that."

"Yeah, I know. Shit. Tell me what to do guys. I'm kind of freaking out over here because he hasn't said a damn thing to me today and what if she told him? What if he knows but he's not telling me he knows?"

Milo shrugs. "Maybe he would be okay with it because it's Hawken. Dex adores you."

Quinton shakes his head, unsure. "Do you want to put your friendship to the test right here, right now?"

"Fuck no!"

Zeke swipes his towel down his sweaty face before hanging it around his neck. "Did she kiss you back?"

"Uh, at first, yeah."

"And then?"

"And then she stopped it. And the night kind of... fizzled. And then I left."

Quinton winces, hissing through his teeth. "Yikes. That bad huh?"

"What? No. It was gr...wait, why am I even telling you all this?"

"You can't help it man. You sampled the forbidden fruit."

"So that's it then? You kissed and that was it?"

"That's it."

Milo cringes. "No phone call? You haven't talked since? Nothing?"

I shake my head. "Nothing." A wave of nausea hits me and my shoulders fall. "Shit. I fucked up, right? I fucked it up with her, didn't I? And now I've fucked it up with her and Dex. What am I supposed to do now?"

"Gentlemen," Colby announces quietly while Dex continues to grunt through his weight training. "I think our buddy Hawken here has a crush."

"So cute," Quinton sings.

"Fuck you very much for your help, guys. I really appreciate it." This is why I didn't want anyone to know, but dammit my head is fuzzy and I'm all out of whack when it comes to thinking about Rory. I'm not at all in my right mind and I need to get myself back on track before I step on the ice because I refuse to be the reason we lose tonight.

Milo laughs quietly. "Look, there isn't much we can do here except keep your secret for you because we certainly don't want Dex knowing about this until the season is over lest he ground your nuts to a pulp and sprinkle them in Colby's Lucky Charms. The rest is up to you. If you want something to happen with Rory, you need to talk to her. If the kiss meant nothing and you want to move on from it, you need to talk to Rory. Either way, Rory is the key."

"It didn't mean nothing," I tell them. "Not to me anyway."

Zeke grins with a sparkle in his eye like a proud father. "Then I'm going to guess you proooobably will kiss again at some point. Better make it worth it when that happens."

"Better make what worth it?" Dex asks after pulling out an earbud and grabbing a drink of water. "What are you pussies all jabbing about over there?"

I try not to flinch at his questioning and look to the guys for a little help. Zeke winks at me and answers, "Tonight's game asshat. I just told Hawken here he better be making all this fucking taint sweat on the bike seat worth it tonight when we own game four."

"A-fucking-men." Dex laughs and then shakes his head. "Then I'm getting my ass home to my girls. Being away from them is really starting to piss me the fuck off. I need to get laid."

Two periods in and we're behind New York by one goal. Zeke has had a hell of a game keeping them out of his net for as much as they've tried, which can only mean one thing. Our defense is sore tonight. We've got to pick it up if we have any chance to win this. I've got to get in there and score to give Dex a reprieve. Once I'm back on the ice for my shift, I meet Quinton's eye and nod as we silently vow to buckle down and get this fucking puck in the net.

At the next faceoff, Milo shoots the puck and it's picked up by Quinton who moves it down the ice. Kurt Harkovic of New York is hot on his trail so he flips and sends the puck blindly my direction but I'm ready for it. I take the open shot I think I have but their goalie denies the in and now I've got to try for round two. I want to stay out of the traffic so the puck doesn't get lost in the shuffle but that's hard to do with ten other guys vying for the same piece of rubber I'm going for.

I lose my footing a bit when I'm hip checked into the wall by Morkowski, forcing me to watch New York take control back to their zone. They try once, twice, three times to get the puck in the net but Zeke is a fucking steel barrier and doesn't let any of their shots get through.

"That'a boy, Miller!" I call out even though he can't hear me.

I hear Dex's voice call out to me and I zone in on his efforts to steal the puck and pass it to me. I'm finally able to get some separation as I sprint down the ice and hit the puck with my backhand, sending it over to Quinton who is out in front of the net where everyone is puck watching. He curls around the puck and just before pushing off to his right, he shoots his shot and fucking SCORES!

"FUCK YES!" I'm the first one on Shay, throwing my arms around him and hugging the shit out of him. "We did it man! One more! Let's fucking go!"

The rest of our teammates surround Quinton with

their high fives, hugs, and cheers and suddenly the energy around us changes.

"Let's fucking get this done and get home, gentlemen!" Colby shouts. "This game is ours for the taking!"

We took home the win we needed and soon we'll be on to the third round of playoffs. The guys are in celebration mode on the plane back to Chicago. Colby and Carissa are lucky enough to get to travel together since she's almost always working whenever Nelson is playing. Much to his dismay, she's been busy editing social media videos since we boarded. He's tried to make out with her a few times but she just pushes his face away and laughs. Watching him pout over her makes me laugh, but inwardly, I'm jealous.

"If you want something to happen with Rory, you need to talk to her. If the kiss meant nothing and you want to move on from it, you need to talk to Rory. Either way, Rory is the key."

I've never really been interested in anything more than a fun time with a woman and I've certainly had my fair share over the years, but lately there's only one woman on my mind and she's probably curled up in bed right now dreaming about...

Oh shit.

Is she playing with The Hawk?

Fuuuck yeah, I bet she is.

Because we won tonight!

She has to be celebrating too, right?

Hopefully alone...in her bed.

I lean my head back on my seat and close my eyes trying to envision what it might be like to watch her get herself off to the toy she's named after me.

"Why do you call it The Hawk, Ror?"

She lifts her head from the back of her yellow chair, her slender, soft legs parted for my viewing pleasure. "Did you know a hawk can see one hundred feet away?" she breathes. "And they see with remarkable clarity."

I lick my lips, her swollen pink pussy glistening for me. "Yeah?"

"Mhmm. You know what that means?"

"What does it mean?"

She takes the Hawk in her hand and slides it along her slit until it lands directly over her clit. "It means The Hawk never misses. He hits the spot every time, Hawken."

"I won't miss, Rory. I'll never fuckin' miss. Just let me taste you. Eat you. Devour you. Savor you. Worship you."

She spreads her legs, hanging each one over the arm of the chair, and fuck me, she is a sight to be seen. "Fuck, you're beautiful like this, Rory."

"What are you waiting for, Malone? Eat me like I'm your very last supper."

"What the fuck are you grinning at?"

"Huh?"

My eyes open and I come back to reality as Dex plops down in the seat next to me. We've never not been seat mates and because the playoffs thrive on superstitions, we can't choose now to sit with someone else lest our luck run out so here I am. Seated next to the brother of the woman I was just fantasizing about.

"I said what are you grinning about? You have this...I don't know, you look like Summer when she has gas."

"Well, that's because I just farted against your seat, bro."

"Shut up. You did not. I don't smell a thing."

I blurt out a laugh. "Nah. I was just thinking about your sister naked and waiting for me."

His head snaps and his eyes bulge. "What the fuck did you just say?"

I wink and laugh at him. "Got ya."

He shakes his head and then punches my upper arm. "Dude, you better never let her hear you say that out loud. She'll tear your shriveled up balls straight from the sac and use them as marble shooters in her classroom."

"That's...an oddly specific thing to do with a man's balls. Have you been thinking about that one a while?"

Dex chuckles. "Nah. I just said the first thing to come to mind."

"Your mind is warped, man."

"Truth. But I bet that would've made Rory laugh."

"Let's see, shall we?" I pull my phone from my pocket and bring up Rory's name in my contacts.

"What?" Dex asks. "You're telling her?"

"Sure am."

ME

> Hey! Dex says if any of us guys talk about you, you'll tear our balls from our nutsacks and use them as marble shooters in your classroom.

RORY

LOL he's right! Better not be talking smack about me, Hawk!

"See? Told ya, dumbass."

"Indeed. She's just as warped as you are."

"Sorry not sorry. But you remember her screaming at me at the housewarming party, right?"

"Uh, how could any of us forget about that? She wanted your balls in a jar, my friend."

He nods. "She knows I mean well."

"We all do. Sooo does that mean you're going to let her date a teammate if she wants to?"

"Pfft! Fuck no." He shakes his head with a scoff. "Besides, I think she wants to find someone who doesn't really care about hockey, you know? She's over it. Plus, she's basically like a sister to everyone here by now anyway. That would just be gross." Dex laughs and sits back in his seat, pulling out his phone and texting Tatum.

A sister?

No fucking way do I view Rory Foster like a sister.

I have two sisters of my own and she is not them.

But at least now I have my in with Rory. The perfect ice breaker text from her brother that will allow me to continue a conversation with her. I just have to make sure I keep it away from Dex.

ME

Just telling him what an excellent dancer you are.

RORY

👀 you did NOT tell him we danced.

ME

What if I did?

RORY

Did you???

ME

Would you want me to?

RORY

Not particularly.

ME

Why?

RORY

I don't have a good answer for that.

ME

What if I told him I kissed you?

RORY

Is he still sitting next to you?

ME

Yeah.

RORY

Then you didn't tell him.

ME

LOL true. I'd probably end up with my head in a toilet.

RORY

Most likely. But it's your life so you know, may the odds be in your favor and all…

At least now I know for sure she didn't tell him.

> ME
>
> I would never do that to you, Ror.

RORY

Can I ask you something?

> ME
>
> Anything.

RORY

Why did you kiss me?

Okay, so we're putting things out there. I can do that.

> ME
>
> I wanted to.

RORY

Oh.

> ME
>
> Can I ask you something?

RORY

I guess?

> ME
>
> Why do you have a sex toy named The Hawk?

RORY

...

RORY

...

> ME
>
> Rory?

> RORY
>
> What's that? *fshshshfshsh*
>
> RORY
>
> Can't hear you.
>
> RORY
>
> Going through a tunnel.
>
> RORY
>
> *fshhfshhsfhsh* Connection is fuzzy.
>
> RORY
>
> Oh well. Guess I'll go to bed now.
>
> RORY
>
> Goodnight!

Fuck.

She's not going to make this easy. I suppose the fact she isn't answering me or telling me I'm full of shit should make me feel slightly better because it tells me I'm not wrong, but in reality, it only makes things worse in my head. She named that toy after me and I need to know why.

She gets herself off thinking of me.

And that thought stirs things in me I should not be considering.

Especially sitting right next to Dex.

Why did you kiss me?

I close my eyes and reread her question over and over again in my head, answering it a different way every time.

"I've wanted to kiss you for a long time."

"It was a spur of the moment decision."

"Because you looked positively radiant in that moment."

"Because dancing with you made me happy."

"Because I think you're beautiful and I like you."

"Because I was dying to know what part of you tasted like."

Christ. This plane needs to land. She's all I've thought about the entire flight and I know damn well I won't sleep tonight until I get an answer out of her. Guess I'm making a pit stop on the way home.

8

RORY

If there's one thing I love about living in this penthouse, it's the view. With the days getting longer, I can see the lakeside out my bedroom windows, but from the living room, I can see the chaotic excitement of the city at night. It's like living in two different worlds with the ability to choose my aesthetic to match my mood.

I don't hate it.

You know what else I don't hate?

Standing in the shower letting the hot water run over my body while I grin to myself replaying my last text conversation with Hawken a couple hours ago.

Why do you have a sex toy named The Hawk?

So, he did see it that night.

He never said a thing about it, but now I know I'm not crazy.

I didn't move The Hawk that night. He did.

But also, shiiiiiit! He knows.

Gah! He knows I've stuck that beautiful purple toy inside me while thinking of him.

He knows I've gotten myself off to thoughts of him.

And because stupid me left it on my chair, he clearly knows I've done it recently.

What am I supposed to do about that?

What was I supposed to say tonight?

No way in hell can I tell him the truth.

I'm going to see him again at their next game. There will be no hiding from Hawken. I'm going to have to come up with a really good lie because how do you tell your brother's best friend that you think he's one of the hottest guys you've ever seen and you fantasize about him doing all kinds of kinky shit to you so you nicknamed your favorite vibrator after him?

Ugh.

I grab my bottle of water and my book from the living room so I can snuggle up in bed and read until I fall asleep. After Charlee's last book recommendation, I've started living in my literary hockey era soaking in all the hockey smut I can.

"Alright gentlemen. How are y'all going to fuck this girl's brains out tonight?"

God, what if this was my real life?

I toss my book onto my pillow and grab my favorite sleepshirt from the foot of the bed. Smiling as I pull the soft fabric over my head, I remember the day I got this shirt and decided it would become the one I sleep in the most.

"Hey man! What are you doing here? Shouldn't you be on a plane home for Christmas?" Dex holds the door open, welcoming Hawken inside. For a split second I feel bad that

I'm sitting here in my pink and red footie pajamas wrapped up on the couch with a chocolate milk mustache but what else does one do when they watch Elf?

"Yeah." Hawken nods. "I have to be at the airport in a little over an hour, but I wanted to make sure I delivered your presents before I left town. I'm sorry I won't be here to celebrate with you two."

"What?" Dex's brow furrows. "Dude, you never have to bring presents here. You know that." His frown turns into a smirk. "But I'm glad you stopped by because it just so happens, I do have something for you."

Hawken laughs. "See asshole? If I would've come here empty handed, I would've felt like a shmuck. Hey, Rory."

"Hi Hawken. Merry Christmas."

"Merry Christmas to you too. Watching Elf again, eh?"

"Don't judge me," I giggle. "It's Christmas break and I'm indulging in my inner child."

He shakes his head with a soft laugh. "No judgement here. You look adorable as always." He lifts a package from his arms and hands it to me. "I got you something."

My brows shoot up in surprise. "Wait, me? You got me something?"

"Yeah. I did."

"Why?"

"Uh, because I wanted to?"

"Hawken..." I tilt my head about to tell him he shouldn't have done that, but he raises his hand in defense.

"Trust me. I think you'll like it. And I promise I didn't go overboard."

"I mean what's overboard to a millionaire exactly?" I wink and he laughs.

"Touché. Just open it smartass."

I rip open the cute wrapping paper and lay a white extra-large shirt box on the couch between us. When I lift the lid and pull back the tissue paper, a huge smile spreads across my face.

"No, you didn't!"

"Sure did."

I lift the Chicago Red Tails hockey jersey from the box, already smiling at the last name written across the back. M-A-L-O-N-E.

"Hawken!" I squeal. "I can't believe you did this! You know I could've just gone and purchased someone else's for myself."

He lifts a shoulder. "Yeah, I know. But now you don't have to whine about only having your brother's name and number to wear. And I have a hundred jerseys, so. There you go."

I hug it to my body and then slip it on over my head, modeling it over my footie pjs.

"What do you think?"

"I think your brother is going to hate it and I'm going to enjoy that laugh."

"Hate what?" Dex asks as he finally walks back into the room, a package under his arm. "Oh, fuck no! What's that piece of garbage?"

Hawken throws his head back in laughter. "See? I told you!"

"Your best friend just saved me from having to wear my own last name to every fucking game, Dexter!"

"There's a t-shirt in there too." Hawken gestures to the box. "So now you have two things to wear."

"She's not wearing that shit, bro," Dex teases.

"Oh yes SHE is," I tell him, spinning around in my new favorite hockey jersey. "Thank you so much, Hawken!" I reach over to hug him and when he wraps his arms around me I get a good whiff of his cologne and holy hell. Whatever it is, it ups his sex factor by like...a gazillion.

Mmm! Gimme more of Hawken Malone.

"Merry Christmas, Rory."

"Merry Christmas Hawken."

I've worn that jersey more times than I can count, and I've slept in this very t-shirt he gifted me ever since. Even on my worst dates, Hawken has been here. Wrapped around me while I sleep. It's silly, probably, but wearing this shirt to bed has always made me feel loved.

I pull the covers back on my bed, about to slip inside to read, when I hear someone knocking on my front door.

Glancing quickly at the clock, I narrow my brow. "It's fucking midnight. Who the hell?"

Maybe it's just Dex being nice and knocking rather than scaring me by waltzing in here late at night when I'm usually sleeping.

Knock, knock, knock.

As quietly as possible I reach up to my tiptoes and peer out the peephole of the door.

"Hawken?"

I unlock the door and swing it open. "Hawk? What's goi—"

He doesn't give me one second to ask what's going on before his lips crash against mine and he's walking me inside, kicking the door closed behind him.

Holy hell, is this a dream?

"You didn't answer me." For every step he takes, I'm forced back until my body is firmly pressed against the hallway wall.

"Answer...what?"

His forehead connects with mine in the darkened space and I can feel his mouth open, breathing against my lips. Brushing against them so gently I almost forget to breathe myself. His tongue slides effortlessly along my bottom lip and fuck if my stomach doesn't immediately fill with butterflies.

"Why did you name your vibrator after me?"

My heartrate skyrockets, but my heart itself drops to the very pit of my stomach.

"Wha-what-what do you mean?"

His eyes are heated and his breathing is slow and deceptively even. "You know damn well what I mean, Ror. I want to know."

His hands push through my hair as he cups my face and kisses me hard. His tongue swipes through my lips tasting me, claiming me. "I *need* to know."

"Why?" I breathe, trying with all my might to remain in control but fuck, this man just walked into my home all confident and sexy and is trying to take what he wants and oh, my God, does it do things to my girly bits.

"Don't fuck with me, Rory," he says against my ear, his hand dropping to my ass. His fingers playing with the hem of my t-shirt. "You know I'm not leaving until you tell me and...fuck, you're not wearing pants."

"It's midnight, you turd. I was about to get in bed."

"I can't get you out of my fucking mind, Rory," he mumbles in between kisses. "Do you know how uncomfortable it is to sit next to your brother on a plane while I fantasize about what his sister might be doing naked and alone in her room?"

A chuckle escapes my mouth as I finally feel like I'm gaining the upper hand. "Wouldn't you like to know?"

He hitches one of my legs up and around his waist, pressing me against the wall with his pelvis and fuuuuuck I can feel him. He slides his hand up my thigh and underneath my panties, gripping my ass, his fingers brushing like feathers against my inner thigh. God, he's right there.

"Yeah, Ror," he says when I gasp at his heated touch. "I really want to know."

"Hawken..."

"Tell me you don't want this, Rory, and I'll stop," he breathes. "I'll step back and walk out that door and we'll never speak about this again."

Fuck. Of course, I want this.

I want this so badly I can taste it.

But it's not that easy.

"Hawk, it's—"

"Ooor, you can tell me why you've given the most impressive vibrator I've ever seen, my name, and in return, I can make every one of your goddamn dreams come true."

His fingers feather between my legs a second time, his reward evident in his moan the moment he slips through my arousal. "Mother fucking...Christ, you're wet for me."

Fuck it.

He's here.

I'm here.

And now I'm horny as hell.

What Dex doesn't know won't hurt him.

"You have that effect on me a lot."

"Do I?"

Catching my bottom lip between my teeth, I fist his shirt in my hands and pull him as close to me as I can possibly get him and then whisper, "Take me to my room, Hawken."

Zero hesitation.

Hawken lifts me up and I wrap my legs around his waist, taking control of his mouth and pulling his hair as he walks us down my familiar hallway. Once in my room, he lets my body slip down until my feet are safely on the floor.

"Show me."

"Show you what?"

"I want to watch you," he tells me. "Get The Hawk and show me. And when you're done, I'm going to devour your swollen sweet pussy like I'm a man who hasn't had a meal in weeks."

That's it.

It's settled.

I couldn't be more turned on if I tried.

I've never heard Hawken Malone talk like this. I've never seen this side of him, but holy shit do I like what I hear. From the shelf underneath my bedstand, I pull out the white box that holds The Hawk, tip the lid and remove my favorite pleasure toy. I start to climb on to my bed but Hawken shakes his head.

"Huh uh." He gestures to my yellow chair. "There."

My brow peaks. "The chair?"

He nods.

"Why?"

"Because I said so." Gah! He says it with such a straight

face, I wonder for a minute if he's some sort of dominant. Regardless, we're in this. There's no turning back now. I want to please him.

"Alright." I step over to my chair and slowly shimmy out of my panties, leaving me in my favorite Red Tails t-shirt. The one with Hawken's last name written across the back.

"Shirt on? Or off?"

"On." His jaw ticks as he watches me and God do I wish I knew what he was thinking.

Seated in my comfy yellow chair, I bring my feet up to the cushion so I can easily spread my legs.

"More," he orders. "Hang them over the sides."

I do as he asks, now positioned spread eagle against the chair and bared open for him. "Like this?"

He brings a hand down his face and shakes his head in disbelief. "Fucking beautiful."

With a push of a button, I turn The Hawk on to its lowest setting, providing a gentle vibrating hum. I try to keep my gaze on the sexy hot hockey player watching from a few feet away, but when the vibrations murmur through my skin, my eyes roll back and my mouth falls open. I inhale a deep breath as the pleasure rolls through me.

"Mmm yeah." I bite my bottom lip. "So good."

With the tap of another button, the shaft begins a slow swivel. I catch Hawken's stare and hold his gaze as I guide The Hawk inside me, stretching me, filling me.

"Fuuuuuck, yes."

Slowly at first I pull the smooth silky toy out and then slide it back in, repeating the movement two, three, four times as my body builds to the pulse of the swivel. Until I can feel my body pulsing with it. And then I tap the next button.

"Oh, God, Hawken. Yesss," I moan audibly as the power surges through the vibrator, massaging my insides in the most glorious ways. "Need more. Want more."

He watches as I bring my hand to my breast and pinch my own nipple, twisting it and tugging it between my fingers as I push the vibrator farther inside me. It's deep enough now that the sucking mechanism can cover my clit and when it does, I start to lose all semblance of control.

"Fuuuuuck!" My chest heaves, my mouth opens, and my eyes roll back in my head at the extreme pleasure building inside my body. And for as much as this damn toy makes me feel like the sexiest person in the room, it's nothing compared to the man standing five feet away from me watching every move I make. Listening to every sound that comes from my mouth. The man who looks like he's about to lose control himself.

He makes me feel like I'm the sexiest person he's ever seen.

And he doesn't even know it.

"Hawken!" I cry out. "Yes! Fuck! I'm going to come."

He's on his knees in front of me in a matter of seconds. "Rory Foster you're the sexiest goddamn thing I've ever laid eyes on, but you will not even think about coming until I'm done with you. Do you understand me?"

My breathing is sporadic and I'm breaking out into a sweat. My head falls back against the chair. "Hawken!"

"This pussy is mine. All fucking mine. Say it."

"It's yours," I pant. "Please, God. It's yours, Hawk."

"That's my girl." He wraps his hand around the

vibrator pulsing inside me. "Both hands on the back of the chair. Hold on and don't let go."

Trying to nod, I lift my hands above my head and grab onto the back of the chair. With the vibrator still running, Hawken turns it so he can reach my clit with his tongue, flicking it relentlessly and then sucking until I'm gasping and desperate for a release.

"Let's see what this thing can do, shall we?" He clicks on the last two buttons and the speed doubles, turning my insides to mush as my inevitable release coils tight.

"Hawken!" I cry out, writhing in the chair as he watches, his hand holding firm as he thrusts The Hawk inside me over and over again, a relentless nonstop assault of pleasure setting me on fire.

"Do you want to come, Ror?"

"Yes!"

"Good. I want every last drop of your cum on my lips." With that, he continues his movements until I can't hold out anymore and I'm screaming his name while parts of me explode and I come so hard, my body shakes. Hawken turns off the vibrator and tosses it to the floor and then my hips are in his hands and he's lifting me like a bowl in a China shop, his soft lips on my swollen, dripping pussy. His tongue lavishly licking every drop my body has to give and before I can stop myself, I'm coming a second time.

"Ooooh...God! Hawk!" I squeal and moan.

"Fucking delicious, Lady Bug."

Lady Bug.

There it is again.

He's called me that before.

And for some reason right now, in this moment, it feels so...intimate.

Personal.

Is this Heaven?

Am I dead?

Because Hawken Malone is eating me out and the mere vision of him in front of me, with his face buried between my legs, is enough that I could die right now and I would die one hell of a happy and satisfied woman.

"Stay right here."

Hawken stands and walks into my bathroom with my vibrator in his hand. He turns on the sink for a minute and then he's back in front of me with a warm washcloth cleaning me up. "You are incredible."

Still trying to catch my breath, I give him a satiated smile. "That's the first time I've ever done anything like that."

"Like what? You've certainly used a toy before."

"Not in front of someone else."

He glances up at me with my panties in his hands. "Well for what it's worth I could watch you do that every single night for the rest of eternity and never get bored. You and your sweet pussy will live rent free in my brain for the rest of my life."

He helps direct my legs into my panties and shifts them up my legs and then he's lifting me from my yellow chair, carrying me to my bed and tucking me in underneath the covers. "Thank you for tonight," he says placing a soft kiss to my forehead. "I'll see you tomorrow?"

What?

"You're leaving?"

He nods. "Practice tomorrow."

"I know, but..." My brows narrow in confusion. I don't understand. "You're not staying here?"

"I have an early morning at the gym. But I knew I wouldn't be able to sleep tonight unless I saw you." His eyes slip down my body. "All of you."

A shy smirk plays across my lips. "But you didn't see all of me."

"Hmm." He huffs a light chuckle. "Next time then." He leans down and kisses my lips, this time an endearingly sweet but chaste pass of his lips over mine. "Good night, Rory. I'll set the alarm on my way out."

A completely unfamiliar set of emotions washes over me as I watch Hawken walk out my bedroom door.

An emptiness as he walks away.

Sadness that he's not staying here with me.

Bereft of his company, his protection.

But at the same time, giddy that he showed up in the first place.

Blissful over what he was able to do to my body.

And exhausted.

Phew! That man is a lot to take in.

I think I could be in trouble with this one.

9

HAWKEN

Once again, Rory is playing hard to get and it's frustrating as hell. With her end of the school year schedule and my need to focus on gameplay I haven't gotten to see her. It's eating at me that I haven't been able to follow up in person after the night I stopped by her place and asked her about The Hawk. In retrospect, I still never got a solid answer from her, but I'll take the way she screamed my name when she came on my tongue as answer enough for now.

God knows I've replayed that night over and over again in my head more times than I ever should. She was an unbelievable sight for sore eyes all sprawled out for me, and she did everything I asked of her. I don't think I could dream up a moment like that if I tried. And who needs porn these days when I can lie in my bed and think about what Rory Foster tastes like?

What she smells like.

What she sounds like when she comes.

Yeah. She's amazing and I'm addicted.

And fucking hell, if Dex knew, I would be a dead man.

Lucky for me, he's been laser focused on his job these past two weeks. We just barely took the first two games of this round and the end is in sight. We're taking it all the way this year. We'll be hoisting the cup over our heads in no time as long as we continue to play a focused and clean game.

Rory and Tatum missed the first game of this round because of a parent night performance at their school, and then game two was on the road. Tonight will be the first time in the last five days I'll get to see Rory face to face and it's all I've been thinking about. We've only spoken via text a few times this week and nothing heavy has come from any of those conversations. She hasn't mentioned my visit and now I'm almost afraid to bring it up.

What if she's not happy with me?

What if she's pissed?

Surely, she understands my schedule and that timing has not worked in our favor.

My phone dings just before I walk out the door to head to the arena.

RORY

Good luck tonight!

ME

Hey Lady Bug! Still coming?

RORY

Wouldn't miss it! Our seats are right next to the sin bin! I'm super pumped to watch the action!

> **ME**
>
> I'll keep an eye out for you. 😊

> **RORY**
>
> You keep your eye on the puck, Malone.
> No excuses! 👀

> **ME**
>
> Yes, ma'am. Pringle's after?

> **RORY**
>
> I imagine so! We'll meet you all in the
> tunnel afterward.

> **ME**
>
> Sounds good. See ya tonight!

"HUSTLE, HIT, AND NEVER QUIT!" we shout together in the tunnel before taking the ice. I have never experienced a crowd roaring so loudly in my life. Talk about an adrenaline rush. We skate out onto the rink, circling around the net as our hometown fans go wild. It's a sea of red in the arena with every fan waving the Red Tails towel they all received as a gift tonight. After I make a few passes, I look toward the sin bin and spot Rory, Charlee, Carissa, and Tatum all seated on the other side of the glass. Well, okay, none of them are seated now. They're all up slapping the glass and cheering us on. It's never really had an effect on me before, seeing the ladies here to cheer on the team. It's just always been what they do. But tonight, Rory Foster is wearing my number. And it's my name she has across her back. She's worn the same jersey since I gave it to her a couple years ago, but now, after last week, it means something to me. Maybe it shouldn't, but it does. I make eye contact with her for a split second but it's enough for her to pass me a wink and seductive smirk that if I think too much about, I'll be uncomfortable in this uniform in no time.

"The fuck!" Dex shouts, skating up to me. My eyes grow huge and I feel myself start to sweat thinking he saw Rory wink at me, but then he gestures to the group of rowdy men jumping around behind the ladies. "They better not lay a hand on the girls or so help me…"

I shake my head and smile at Dex's overprotective nature. "Relax man. They're right down front. They're safe. Besides, I'm damn sure any one of those ladies can hold their own against any drunk bastard at a hockey game. This isn't their first rodeo." I pat my teammate on the back as Tatum blows him a kiss and then we're off to get ready for the first faceoff.

Halfway through the second period we're up three to one. It's been a night full of action and the energy grows higher with every passing minute. The crowd appreciates the spirited play from both sides. Shay tracks down the latest pass from Landric. Dex is out on defense at the moment against Boulder's Mitch Landerson who lost the puck when he tried to make a move. A battle ensues in the corner between Landerson, Colby, and Dex, who victoriously get the puck right out in front and I'm ready for it. I don't hesitate for a second and hit the puck into the net. The crowd is on their feet, their shouts of celebration reaching near deafening levels.

"Fuck yes, Malone!" Dex wraps his arms around me in celebration. "That's how it's fucking done, my man!"

The rest of the guys all crowd around me for a group hug before game play continues. Out of the corner of my eye, I catch Rory and the girls jumping up and down cheering us on and I can't hold back my smile. With any luck, we'll take the win for this game and I'll end the night with Rory in my arms.

And if I'm really lucky, in my bed.

The third period proves more difficult as Boulder scores twice bringing the score to four-three Red Tails. We're still ahead, but it's getting a little close for my liking and if the looks of anger and drive on the faces of my teammates mean anything, they all feel the same way.

"Dig in, gentlemen! Bring it home," Coach Denovah shouts from behind us. "Landric, Shay, Malone, Foster, show them how we take what's ours."

We hit the ice for our next shift and almost immediately Foster is hip checked into the wall by Kurt Windel.

"Watch yourself fucking prick!" I shout at him as I position myself next to Dex.

"What's the matter Malone? You gettin' scared?" He laughs as he wins the puck from our battle and passes to his teammate.

Fucking pig fucker.

The puck is on the move and we're sprinting down the ice to regain control. Boulder's Landerson tries to move past Zeke but he shuts him down and passes to Shay. As I skate past the sin bin, I catch a glance of the ladies shouting at the men behind them but can't allow myself to focus on them.

They're fine.

Get the fucking puck, Malone.

Shay takes the puck back across the ice and around the net before passing to Landric who takes a shot but it ends up off the back glass, the Boulder crowd cheering on their goalie. Boulder desperately needs this next goal if they want to stay in the game and they'll do just about anything to give themselves the advantage. Dex gets an icing call and Shay gets tripped up by Boulder's Wingerson. Colby's on the bastard in a hot second of retaliation.

"Son of a bitch!"

The crowd amps up as the two begin to fight. Hands slapping on the glass around us and shouts from both sides can be heard all around. It's chaos in the arena as both teams are desperate for this win. I watch as Colby is checked against the glass again and turn around just in time for my heart to plummet into my stomach. The group of guys seated behind Rory have started fighting, and one of them is punched, causing him to fall forward against Rory who in turn gets pummeled into the glass. Her head ricochets off the wall, her nose spurting with blood on contact.

"Rory!"

She covers her face and the ladies try to help her and here I am, stuck on the ice playing this fucking game with a bunch of unprofessional, dirty players. I'm helpless.

"Fuck!"

The refs separate Nelson and Wingertson and the play continues with Landric winning the next faceoff and passing to Shay, but all I can focus on is Rory's bloodied face. I have to get to her.

Have to check on her.

Sin bin!

Sprinting down the ice, I get as close as I can to Landerson, pretending to go after the puck but I don't give two shits about the puck right now. I need to get to Rory, so I hold out my stick and cross check Landerson knowing damn well what will happen. The ref calls my penalty and sends me to the sin bin for a two-minute Boulder power play.

Yes!

I skate off in the direction of the penalty box and once there, I knock on the glass right next to where there is now medical staff helping Rory.

"Rory!"

Nobody answers me.

There's blood on her face and splattered on her jersey and she's favoring her left arm.

Fuck!

I slap on the glass with both hands this time.

"Charlee! Is she okay? Rory!"

Finally, Carissa looks up and then tells Rory I'm here. Her head snaps up to where I'm seated on the other side of the glass. I press my hand firmly against the barrier between us.

"Are you alright?"

She nods, holding her nose with one of the girls' Red Tails towels. She presses her free hand opposite mine on the glass. "I'm okay. I'll be fine and what the fuck are you doing?"

"Wait, what?"

"That was a blatant cross check, Hawken! You did that on purpose."

"Fuckin' right I did." I don't need to tell her why. My eyes say it all for me. I care about Rory and it freaked me the fuck out to see her hurt. I needed to make sure she was okay.

"Hawken..." Her shoulders fall and her eyes start to water, but I can't have her crying now. I'll never get through the rest of the game.

"Ror, please don't cry." I turn to look back at the ice knowing my two minutes are almost up. "I've got to...Ror, it's okay. You're going to be okay."

"We'll take her downstairs and meet you there after the game," Carissa says. "I'll get Rashad to check her out."

"Fuck no!" Rory shakes her head. "We're watching the end of this game." She points to me. "Now you get your ass back out there and do your job, Malone or so help me..."

God, this girl.

Bloody nose and a semi black eye and all she cares about is her team pulling out the win.

"Yes ma'am!" I wink at her quickly and then my two minutes are up and I'm back on the ice sprinting toward Quinton to help him bring this game to a close.

"She alright, man?" I hear Landric ask when I speed past him.

I join the battle in the corner and manage to hit the puck away where it's saved by Zeke and sent back up the ice.

"She's a fuckin' warrior, that one," I tell him with a shake of my head on my next pass. Out of the corner of my eye I see Wingerson moving closer to me, but I leave him no room to get in my way. I position myself just to the side of their net as the puck passes between my teammates. It's turned over for just a moment by Landerson but I'm on him for the steal and then turn and shoot into the upper net for the final goal of the game.

The crowd goes wild as the clock ticks down and we know this game is ours. I glance toward the penalty box just in time to see the ladies heading up the stairs, Rory still holding the towel to her face and Charlee holding her arm. I've never wanted to get off the ice as fast as I do now.

"What the fuck happened?" Dex asks when he, Milo, and I stop into Rashad's examination room to see Rory lying on his table, Charlee holding her hand. He's one of the best medics on our staff. I would trust him with my life, so I know Rory is in good hands.

"Don't worry about it, Dex. I'm fine."

I have to bite my tongue not to chuckle because with blood on her face and splattered down her jersey, she's so not fine.

Dex's brows narrow. "Uh, news flash Sis, fine does not mean laying on Rashad's table while he tends to a bloody gash in your head."

She scoffs. *"On'tday ebay osay amaticdray."*

"Ouyay otgay ashedsmay intoway away allway."

"Itway asway othingnay!"

Looking between the arguing siblings I roll my eyes.

"Would you two cut it out with the Pig Latin already?"

Dex huffs. "Was this those guys? The ones behind you? I saw them when we first got on the ice, but Hawken here said you all could hold your own with those bastards." He backhands my chest.

"Oh, she handled them just fine," Charlee laughs. "They were drunk Boulder fans who made a pass at her and she clapped the fuck back."

My blood boils. "They made a pass at you? Did they touch you, Ror?"

She shakes her head and cringes forgetting Rashad is still working on her. "No. Well, not until the son of a bitch fell into me and knocked me over."

"What did they say to you?" Dex wants every damn detail like he's going to walk outside and find the assholes who hurt his sister.

"I..." She exhales. "It doesn't matter. I'll be fine. I just have a headache and my arm is sore."

"I don't think this will need stitches," Rashad reports. "I've cleaned it and I'm going to bandage it a little for now, but I expect it'll stop bleeding within an hour or so. If it starts gushing or something, then we'll want to reconsider stitches."

"And her arm?" Dex asks.

"I did a quick x-ray and nothing appears to be broken." He turns to me. "It looks like you strained your rotator cuff when you hit the glass. I would suggest not working it too hard for a couple of days and if it's not feeling better, get in to see your doctor and have it further examined. I could give you a brace to use so you're not tempted to move it too much."

"Thanks Rashad."

"My pleasure."

"Yeah, thanks Rashad." Dex shakes his hand. "I appreciate you taking the time to look at her."

"Anytime my man. Your family is our family." He turns back to Rory and helps her sit up. "You're all set Rory. Continue with Tylenol and Ibuprofen for the pain. Ice on the shoulder. You should be alright in a day or two."

She peers up at the rest of us. "So? We going to Pringle's or what?"

Milo and I laugh but Dex frowns at her and shakes his head. "Fuck no, we're not going to Pringle's. Rory you're injured."

"Okay," she says, rolling her eyes. "But I'm not dead. Geesh. I can handle sitting in a booth for a while. You all deserve to celebrate and I refuse to be the reason that doesn't happen."

"You know I'll take you home if you want, Ror," I tell her.

Dex scoffs. "Not a fucking chance. She's not staying alone tonight. She can come home with me."

"Dex, cut it out, I don't need a nanny."

"Rory you could have a concussion or worse. Someone needs to be with you overnight just in case."

Rory looks to Rashad who bobs his head. "It's not a bad idea. Better safe than sorry."

"Then she can stay at my place," I offer without hesitation. Everyone in the room looks at me like I've just spoken a third language. "What? I literally live one building over so nobody will have to trek across town. Besides, it's not like she hasn't stayed there before. I have plenty of room."

I don't need to mention that I have no intention of letting her sleep alone tonight.

"Fine." Rory huffs with another roll of her eyes. "I'll stay with Hawken, but we're going to Pringle's first."

"And you'll let me know the minute you feel like leaving?"

She nods. "Yes."

"Promise?"

"Ugh yes. Okay? I promise. Now can you guys get cleaned up so we can go? I'm hungry and their sweet potato fries are calling my name."

I manage to slip into the booth just after Rory so she's seated between myself and Zeke. This way I can keep a close eye on her and be right here when she's ready to leave. We order a table full of food that everyone helps themselves to like it's a buffet fit for a group of kings. I even order extra sweet potato fries since Rory mentioned wanting some, but to my knowledge, she's only grabbed a few off the plate. Other than that, she's been sipping from the same glass of water for the past half hour.

"That's going to end up one bad ass looking scar, Rory," Quinton says, gesturing to her forehead.

"Yeah?" Her fingers feather over her bandaged forehead and she winces slightly. "Can it be the shape of the word *fuck*? Because that would be pretty badass."

Tatum laughs. "Right because that would go over so well in your classroom."

"Alright then maybe at least a cool zigzag so the kids can think I'm the next Harry Potter?"

"You'll barely be able to see it once it heals," I tell her with a nudge. "Believe me. Remember last season when Quinton got his cheek sliced by a skate?"

Quinton smooths his hand down his face. "Like a baby's bottom now. The battle wound didn't last long. Oh, and remember Colby a few seasons ago slit his wrists during a game?"

Colby nods. "Oh shit, I remember that game. Fucking idiot came out of nowhere and fell in front of me. Sliced the hell out of my wrist."

"And what did you do?" I ask with a smirk. "You were off the ice for a quick stitch up and back in the game for the last period."

"Hell yeah, I was. I wasn't about to miss my opportunity to get revenge on that douche bag."

"Yeah well, you get paid millions to carry funny looking battle scars. Me on the other hand..."

Dex leans forward, his elbows resting on the table across from Rory. "You gonna tell us what those bastards said to you?"

"*Openay.*" She shakes her head.

"*Ywhay otnay?*"

"Because it doesn't matter, Dexter."

"It fucking matters because you went through shit because of it."

"Aww Dex." She cocks her head. "Is this you trying to be the protective big brother?"

"You know damn well I'd do anything for you, Ror. I'm the fucking reason you were even there tonight in the first place. Your pain is on me."

She rolls her eyes at him for the hundredth time

tonight. "Just forget about it, alright? I'm fine. I'll be fine. It's over."

The conversation moves in a new direction and before long, Rory leans over, resting her head on my shoulder and it's all I can do to not completely overreact and slide my hand around her to hold her against me. Dex eyes her and I look down to see if her eyes are open. They flutter open and closed a few times and I nod to Dex who is starting to show concern.

"I think it's time to take her home," I say quietly to those of us at the table. Sliding my hand to her thigh underneath the table, I lean down and murmur in her ear. "Hey Ror, you ready to go?"

"You stay. I'm fine," she mumbles against me.

"That's cute, Ror." I chuckle lightly. "Let's get you home."

"Do you need help?" Dex asks me, but I shake my head.

"Nah. She just needs to sleep the night off. Her body's tired."

I tap her leg with my hand and tell her it's time to go and then slip out of the booth, helping her out as well. She sways a bit so I wrap an arm around her and give Dex another reassuring nod.

"You okay, Rory?" he asks when she stands.

"Yeah." She nods. "Just a headache."

"I've got what she needs at home," I tell him. "I promise she's in good hands."

"Take care of her, man. Call me if you need anything. I can stop by in the morning or whatever."

"Yeah, I'll text you as soon as she's up."

"Thanks for giving her a place to crash. I appreciate it."
Like I would let her go anywhere else.

10

RORY

"Stay right there. Let me help you." Hawken opens his car door and slips out.

"I appreciate the chivalry, Hawk," I answer even though he's already walking around to my side of the car as I push my door open. "But I think I can manage getting out of the car just fi-uuuuck." Hawken catches me around the waist when I stand from the car and immediately sway.

"Why do you feel the need to be so independent, Rory?" Hawken chuckles as he wraps his arm around me.

"I didn't realize how dizzy I was until..."

"Yeah. Charlee said you hit your head pretty damn hard. For Christ's sake just let me help you. In fact..." He reaches down and positions his arm under me, lifting me from the ground and carrying me in his arms.

"Hawken."

"Just relax and let me get you safely inside, alright?"

He walks us to the elevator inside his parking garage and hits the keycode for his penthouse. In the meantime, as much as I want to fight the need to be carried, I do what he says and lean my head against his chest, relaxing in his hold. He smells good, like whatever soap he uses in the shower, so I close my eyes and simply breathe him in until we make it inside.

He doesn't put me down until we're not only in his penthouse but in his darkened bedroom.

"Hawken what are you doing?"

"You're sleeping with me tonight."

"What?" I lift my head from his chest. "Hawk, that's tot—"

"No arguments, Rory," he insists, finally lowering me to his bed and then reaching over to turn on his bedside light. "You might have a head injury so I'm not leaving you alone tonight. You're sleeping here."

I cock my head. "Is this some sort of...I don't know, fancy way of trying to get into my pants?"

His smirk is so damn adorable, but my headache is preventing me from wanting to smile or show extra emotion whatsoever. "Pretty sure I already accomplished that goal, Rory."

"Doesn't count."

"What?" He laughs.

"Yeah, because I wasn't wearing pants to begin with."

"Semantics," he says with a chuckle as he walks over to his dresser and pulls out a t-shirt. "Here. You can sleep in this if you want. We should get that bloody jersey off you."

Having forgotten all about the blood stains on my shirt, I look down to survey the damage, anguish washing over me. "Hawken, look." I pull at the material. "That's never going to come out. It's ruined."

SUSAN RENEE

He crouches down so he's more at my level. "It's not ruined, Ror. I promise, I'll get it cleaned for you and have it looking like brand new."

"But it won't smell like you anymore."

He sits back, giving me a confused look. "What?"

"I..." I twist my mouth around, not sure that I want to give him this confession. "I've never washed it."

His brows shoot up. "Never?"

I shake my head, my chin trembling. "It smelled like you when you gave it to me and I didn't want that scent to go away." There's a sudden tightness in my chest with my divulgence and I feel a bit stupid for almost crying to Hawken about this. I'm clearly exhausted. "God, I'm sorry," I tell him through a few rebel sniffles. "I'm just exhausted."

"I know you are." He cups my face with his hand and I lean into his warmth. "How about this. Once we get it cleaned again, I'll either wear it for a while or I'll spray it with my cologne so it still smells like me. How does that sound?"

I answer him with a small nod. "Yeah. That would be nice. I'm sorry Hawken. I don't mean to be so stupid emotional. I just have a huge headache."

"I know. Can I help you get dressed so you can relax and sleep? I promise no funny business."

Without answering him, I pull my good arm into my bloodied jersey and try to do the same with the other arm but it hurts more than I anticipate.

"Here. Let me help." Hawken pulls the jersey sleeve out a little so there's more room and helps navigate my arm through the hole. He lifts it over my head and then helps me get out of the long sleeve t-shirt I'm also wearing, leaving me in nothing but my jeans and bra. He clears his throat and I see his Adam's apple bob when he swallows. "Do you need help with..."

I try to reach my arm around to unclasp it myself but the pain radiating through my shoulder has my wincing enough that he stops me. "No. Let me do it. I'll close my eyes so I can't see, alright?"

"They're just boobs, Hawken. I'm fairly sure you've seen boobs before."

He stares at me like he wants to say something but doesn't. Instead, he leans up on his knees in front of me and reaches around to unclasp the back of my bra. His face is so close to mine I could easily kiss him, breathe his breath, and for a minute I consider doing it.

Would he kiss me back?

Would he tell me no?

I'm really not in the mood to be turned down tonight.

And my head really does hurt.

So rather than egg him on or make him feel at all uncomfortable with the fact I'm about to be shirtless in front of him, I hold my breath as he tenderly pulls the straps down each of my shoulders and slides them off my arms.

Yep. I'm naked from the waist up in front of Hawken Malone.

And it's anything but sexual.

Fuck my life.

Except it's also extremely sweet that he's taking care of me like this.

So maybe this isn't so bad.

He grabs the t-shirt from his dresser and pulls it down over my head and then helps my arms through the holes.

"Thank you, Hawken."

"Sure. Let me grab you some pain relievers before you fall asleep."

While he steps into his bathroom, I stand slowly and unzip my jeans, pulling them down with one hand and shimmying out of them. He brings me a few pills and a glass of water which I down right in front of him before handing him the glass and then resting my head against his pillow.

"I'll just be a minute, alright?"

"Mhmm." My eyes are already closing. As much as I wish this night were ending differently, I mean I'm pants-less in Hawken Malone's bed for fuck's sake, I know sleep is inevitable and desperately needed.

Hawken turns out the bedside light and steps into the bathroom quickly before coming to bed. I feel the moment he slides in next to me. Just as he promised me, there's no funny business. No touching of any kind. No attempts to snuggle. I can respect him for not trying to make this experience be something it shouldn't be, but being this close to Hawken in bed and not snuggling up next to him?

Nope.

No way.

No can do.

So, I turn over and lay my head against his chest, resting my injured arm against his abdomen, which is completely bare by the way. I register the quick intake of breath when I touch him, but I'm too close to sleep to say anything about it. Hawken is warm and surprisingly soft for as rock hard as I know his body is. Tonight, he's my pillow.

My healer.

My solace.

My peace.

And right before I drift off, I swear I hear him whisper, "This is my perfect."

I have no idea what time it is when my eyes open again. It could be midafternoon and I would never know it thanks to the blackout curtains in Hawken's bedroom. Regardless of the time, I'm sweating and I feel sticky and gross. Hawken is an exceptional cuddler, but he's hot as hell. Sleeping with him is like being covered in a balmy eighty-degree weighted blanket. That's not to say I hate it. I don't. Not by any means, but after not showering last night and washing the literal blood, sweat, and tears away before going to bed, coupled with not brushing my teeth either, I feel like I've just woken up from having the flu.

There's no way I don't smell like a troll.

I need to shower.

Before moving too much I try to survey my body as much as possible.

No more headache.

My neck isn't sore.

Legs are good.

Don't feel dizzy.

I try to raise my arm up into the air.

Not terrible, but still fairly sore.
Best not to push it.
Got it.

As quietly as possible, I slip out of Hawken's bed, careful not to wake him, and pad into the master bathroom closing the door behind me. His bathroom is nothing short of incredible luxury. I could literally spend hours in here relaxing as I would in any world class spa. Dark walls surround a large white two-person tub situated in front of a working fireplace. Seriously, a fireplace in a bathroom is like a dreamhouse detail for me. I was never able to talk Dex into putting one in and quite frankly, I'm surprised Hawken went for it. Perhaps it was already here when he moved in. The skylights accentuated by the darkened ceiling would add the perfect amount of natural light to the room, but clearly, I'm up earlier than the sun as there is very little daylight coming through at the moment.

To the right of the tub and fireplace is a huge slate colored walk-in shower with two built in benches and more knobs and buttons than I know what to do with. I find the switch for the shower lights and turn them on so I don't send too much light under the door into the bedroom and wake up Hawken. The soft lighting is nice actually. I grab an extra toothbrush from the pile he keeps stored in the medicine cabinet so I can brush my teeth and then grab a towel from the shelf and hang it on the hook next to the shower. Studying the buttons and knobs along the shower wall, I figure out how to turn on the water and whoa!

Multiple shower heads from every direction!

Oh, my God, this might be the best shower I've ever had.

I shimmy out of my panties and gently pull my arm

through my shirt sleeve, a slightly easier task since it's Hawken's shirt and is too big for me as it is.

Stepping under the water feels incredible. The luke-warm droplets stream over my heated skin, washing away the stress of last night. Washing away the stiffness in my body. I thought my shower was amazing when it comes to water pressure but oh, my God, Hawken's is ten times better than mine. A steady stimulation all over my body, it's like standing in an unwavering warm rain shower.

The moan that escapes me might have been a tad louder than it should've been, but who could blame me at this point? I could stand in here all day. There are several bottles of hair and body products situated on a long shelf to my left. Reading them all, I find one with a scent I think I'll like and step forward to grab it, but in doing so, I slip in the water puddled at my feet. I try to catch myself by grabbing onto the marbled shelf but end up pushing every bottle off the edge at the same time.

"Shhhhit! Fuck!" I shout as the bottles go flying, some of them smacking me in the face on the way down. Steadying myself, I lay my head on my arm and remind myself to breathe.

You didn't fall.

You're still alive.

And in one piece.

You can fix the mess.

"Rory?" The door slams open and Hawken comes barging in. "What's going...fuck, Rory, are you alright?"

He doesn't even ask. And I don't say a word before he opens the glass shower door and steps into the heavenly rain with me, wrapping himself around my naked and now very wet body from behind.

"Are you hurt?"

I shake my head.

God, this is humiliating.

"Rory? I need you to look at me. Are you okay?"

His hands are on my shoulders and he's turning me toward him and oh, my God, I am naked here! Completely naked. Yeah, I know. The man ate me out like I was his very last meal not too long ago, and it was the best thing to happen to me in a very long time, but still. I wasn't totally naked then. Squeezing my eyes closed, I allow him to turn me around.

His hands cup my face, his thumbs smoothing over my cheeks. "Rory. Look at me."

When I finally open them, his beautiful hazel eyes are staring at me with more concern than I saw from him even yesterday. "Are you okay?"

"Yeah," I whisper. "Just slipped and tried to catch myself. I'm sorry."

He shakes his head. "Don't apologize. They're just shampoo bottles." He leans down and picks them all up in one fell swoop, depositing them on the shower bench next to us. "What are you even doing up? It's four-thirty in the morning."

My shoulders drop. "I'm sorry Hawken. I woke up sweating and I felt gross and I really just wanted to wash my hair and..." I turn my head. "You have a fucking fire-place in your bathroom."

He cocks his head, a bit befuddled. "Yeah. It's been there for years."

"Well, this is the first time I've ever been in this bathroom, so..." I don't finish the sentence because why bother? He knows I've never been here. "I guess I'm jealous and now I want one in my bathroom."

"You can shower in here whenever you want, Ror."

"I didn't mean to wake you up." Of course, I choose now to cross my arms in front of my body trying to hide myself from him. Don't ask me why. It's four-thirty in the morning and I don't know what the hell I'm really doing.

"Can I wash your hair?" he asks softly, smoothing his hands down the back of my head.

"What?"

He leans over and grabs one of the shampoo bottles. "Your hair. Let me wash it for you."

I shake my head. "Hawken you don't have to d—"

"I want to," he says, squirting shampoo into his hand and lathering it before sliding his strong fingers into my hair. He turns me away from the water and works the soap into my hair, massaging my scalp.

"Mmmm," I groan, relaxing at the feel of his hands in my hair. "That feels so good, Hawk."

"I'm glad you like it."

With his hand on the back of my head, he pulls me forward until my forehead rests on his chest. He slowly massages from my temples to the back of my neck. Beginning to relax, I open my eyes for a quick moment and ho. Lee. Shit.

Hawken has a boner.

And not just a little tent pitching in the black boxer briefs he's still wearing.

No, Sir.

Whatever beast of a cock is in there, it's hulking out and ready to rip through that soft cotton fabric.

I'm staring at Hawken Malone's Hulk-sized boner.

"K. Lean your head back into the water." He guides my head back and turns me just enough so my hair can be rinsed. Once again, he gently massages his fingers through my strands as the soap washes away.

"Hawken?"

"Hmm?" His voice rumbles through his chest.

"You have a boner."

His hands stop moving as does the rest of his body, my eyes popping open in response.

He huffs out a slight chuckle. "What did you expect?"

"What do you mean?"

"I mean, sometimes my dick has a mind of its own, but I'm currently standing in the shower with a beautiful woman and she's naked and soaking wet in front of me."

Ignoring the butterflies now flitting through my stomach, I try to keep a straight face. "So, you're saying your very...uh, large and girthy boner is my fault?"

When I'm finally brave enough to make eye contact with him, the corner of his mouth quirks up. "Something like that." He holds my stare for several long seconds, the two of us breathing in tandem. Honestly, I can't tell if he's moments away from devouring me or if he's trying to deny us both what we know is inevitable.

"Turn around, Lady Bug," he commands.

"Excuse me?"

The heat in his eyes is indescribable. "I said turn around." His hands slide down the wet skin of my back, settling just above my ass, and then he turns me toward the shower wall facing away from him.

"Wh-why? What are you doing?"

He rubs a dollop of shower gel between his palms and I watch as the suds spread over his fingers with anticipation. "Giving the dirty girl what she needs," he says, placing his hands on my shoulders, his strong hands massaging my skin as the suds slide down my back. From behind me, he leans in toward my ear and murmurs, "And torturing my—how did you put it? Large and girthy—boner for a little while longer."

I want to laugh.

I want to make light of his last comment to relieve us both of this ineffable sexual tension, but I can't. The moment his hands touch my body I'm a goner. With every press of his thumbs against my back I melt into him. Every rub of his hands around my neck makes me moan with a newfound relaxed pleasure.

Holy hell if I had only known he could massage like this.

How he can calm the muscles straining in my body and ignite my insides at the same time, I'll never know, but he's doing it. The vanilla and coconut scent emanating from the soap suds is delightful and when he maneuvers his hands down my back, squeezing and kneading my skin, my muscles, my body, I may as well be putty in his hands.

11

HAWKEN

Her beautiful body is warm, soft, and wet beneath my fingers as I make my way down her back. I can tell the moment she finally allows herself to relax in my hands when she melts against me, her head falling to my chest resting just below my shoulder.

"Hawk, this is..." I lift her good arm and massage her bicep, twisting my hands around her arm, pushing and pulling against her skin to relieve her tension. "So nice," she groans. She shifts against me, her ass rubbing along my stiff cock and I inhale a swift breath.

Fuuuck.

"Keep that up, Lady Bug and this early morning pamper session is going to turn into something entirely different."

"Is that so?"

She shifts again, her naked ass practically stroking me. I throw my head back, squeezing my eyes closed and trying extremely hard not to release the hungry beast inside me who very much wants to bend her over and take what I've been craving for longer than I care to admit.

"You don't play fair, Lady Bug," I breathe against her ear. "I'm trying to do the right thing here, Ror, but a man only has so much control. Especially when the one I've fantasized about is naked in front of me, taunting me with her ass against my cock."

"Mmm," she groans, teasing me with a shimmy again. "Your impressively large, rock-hard and...throbbing cock."

Sliding my soapy hands down her back, I wind them around her torso, palming her ribcage and lazily working my way up. She gasps against me, arching her back. Her perfect, glistening wet breasts popping out for my viewing pleasure.

"Is that what you want?" I murmur. "You want to feel my throbbing cock, Rory? You want to feel how fucking hard you make me?"

Her mouth opens and she bites her bottom lip, a soft whimper escaping her. "Hawken..."

"You want to see me lose control? Is that it?" I slide a hand up and over her breast, squeezing it gently in my palm. She gasps louder.

Good God, she's perfection.

My other hand slides down her torso and between her legs, my fingers delving through her delicate softness as she bucks forward. "You want to feel me thrust inside you? Claiming your sweet cunt and filling you with every ounce of my cum?"

"Oh, God. Yes," she whispers.

"Tell me, Rory."

"Yes." Her breathless answer spurs me on.

"Yes, what?" I cross my arms over her chest, both of her breasts in my hands, and then pinch each nipple between my thumb and forefinger.

"I want those things," she cries out. "All of them."

"I need you to say it."

"Fuck me, Hawk," she begs. "Christ, I need you to fuck me."

I pull her tight against me, one hand grasping her breast, the other pushing between her legs as two of my fingers penetrate her. My lips on her neck, I kiss and suck my way up until I catch her earlobe between my teeth.

"Do you know how long I've waited to hear you beg for me, Rory?" I ask, my voice gruff and pained as I pleasure her body. Both of us inhaling and exhaling in tandem.

"Hawken," she gasps. "Why...why didn't you ever say anything?"

"Your brother can be very convincing."

"Yeah?"

"Mhmm." I kiss down her neck and shoulders, my hand roaming from one breast to the other.

"Well, he can also be a very big cock block," she rasps. "So, if we're going to stand here and talk about my brother, you can kindly remove your fingers from my pussy."

I smile against her skin and then teasingly nibble on the base of her neck. "Not a fucking chance. My fingers are right where they want to be." I slide my fingers out of her and rub her swollen clit with a mixture of her arousal and water from the shower. Her knees weaken and she cries out. Her hand grasping at the wall in front of her to steady herself.

"Fuck, Rory. I can't wait to be inside you."

She leans her head back against my shoulder and I pull my fingers from her so I can hold her face in my hands. She immediately turns so that our bodies are flush, the hardened peaks of her nipples brushing against my skin. And then her lips crash into mine in a tongue-thrusting kiss so hungry and scintillating she takes my breath away and I gasp a breath.

"Rory."

I try to claim her lips once more but she's one step ahead of me, peppering my chest with kisses, and then my stomach, my hip. And then she's on her knees pulling my soaked boxer briefs down my legs, freeing my straining erection.

Fuuuucking hell.

This is happening.

She grips me with both hands and runs her tongue over me from root to tip and then swirls her tongue around the head.

"Jesus Christ, Rory." Watching this woman wrap her lips around my cock and suck me into her mouth is a fucking dream come true. She fondles my balls in her hand as she holds the base of my cock with the other, and then she lowers her mouth over my shaft, taking me in inch by inch.

"Oh, shit, Ror. Such a fucking good girl. That's amazing."

So I can get the best view of this gorgeous woman, I gather her wet strands and wrap them around my hand. "God, you're stunning like this. With my cock down your throat, your lips squeezing my shaft, your cheeks hollowing out. Fuck. Take it all, Ror. Let me see how far you can take my cock."

She looks up at me from beneath her long eyelashes, the mischief in her eye telling me she's up for the challenge. The tip of my cock in her mouth, she reaches around to my ass, palming each cheek and pulling me into her, sucking my entire fucking cock into her mouth until I feel the back of her throat. She gags a little but doesn't let that stop her. She continues the action once, twice, three times, each time a little faster.

"Jesus, Rory. God, I've never wanted to fuck a mouth so badly in my life."

She comes up for air, popping off my cock long enough to smirk and say, "Well here's your chance pretty boy. What are you waiting for?"

"Holy shit." I squeeze my eyes closed as she takes me in again, her tongue swirling around my head. "Take my cock, Rory. Take the whole damn thing." My hand wrapped around her hair, I slowly but assertively thrust my cock between her lips while gently guiding her head down to take me all in and she does it with impressive ease. Grabbing my ass, she digs in her nails and sucks me off like the goddess she is, accelerating to a perfect speed.

And. It. Is. So. Fucking. Good.

"Fuck, Rory," I hiss through my teeth. "I'm going to come baby."

She continues back and forth, back and forth, swirl of her tongue, back and forth until I'm almost ready to explode, but instead of letting her swallow my cum, I step back, effectively stopping her. "No. Not like this. I need to be inside you right fucking now."

I lean down and help her stand and then practically lift her from the ground. "Wrap your arms around my neck. Is that okay? You're not hurting too much?"

"It's fine," she pants. "Totally fine."

"Good. This won't take long." I reach between us and find her opening and then without warning I lower her down over top of me, both of us groaning as she stretches around me.

"Hawk! Oh God, it's so good."

"Mother fuck, Ror. Shit. I'm sorry, I need to move."

"Yes! Please!"

I hold her ass and push her down over me as I thrust up as hard and fast as I can because holy shit this woman is everything and her pussy wrapped around my cock is the most incredible thing I've ever experienced.

"Hawk! Yeah! Oh God! Yes! Yes!"

I can't even speak anymore, I'm so laser focused on hitting the right spot, listening to her fucking sensual voice, and reveling in the feeling of Rory Foster's pussy taking me in like it was made for me. Working us both into a frenzy, Rory throws her head back, her mouth open in ecstasy as I pick up my speed and race to the finish line.

"Ooooh God!" she cries as she rakes her nails from the middle of my back to the top of my shoulders. "Fuuuuuck, Hawk! I'm going to come! I can't! I can't! I can't..."

"Come with me, Rory. Be a good girl and come with me."

She screams out one more time and shatters in my arms and I'm right there with her. Emptying myself inside her, holding her against me, hugging her on the outside while she hugs me on the inside. Her arms wrapped tightly around my neck as if she's holding on for dear life and never wants to let go.

Fuck, I would be okay with that.

Don't let go Rory.

Please don't fucking let go.

"Morning, Lady Bug. How are you feeling?" She walks into the kitchen wearing nothing but my t-shirt immediately reaching for a mug and a K-cup of her favorite coffee, which I also keep stocked all the time just in case.

She raises her pointer finger and mumbles, "Coffee first."

Turning back to the eggs I'm cooking on the stove I smile to myself and shake my head. She remains silent until her mug of coffee is completely ready at which point, she lifts it to her lips and takes a sip.

"Ahh," she sighs with a satisfied smile. "How do I feel? Uh, I guess I feel freshly fucked and satisfied in more ways than I can count."

She's not wrong. Three times between four-thirty and six in the morning was an amazing dream come true. I chuckle softly and then turn to place a kiss on her forehead.

"I meant your arm, but I'm glad to hear you're a satisfied woman." I pat her ass and then lift her chin with my finger so I can try to read her eyes. Rory's good at saying things and hiding her true feelings. Sometimes I get her, and I know exactly what she's thinking. Others...well, may the odds please be in my favor.

"Are you sure you're alright? Not too sore?"

"Oh, I'm sore." She nods, a light humor to her voice. "Walking down the hall to get to the kitchen felt a little different this morning. But I promise I'm sore in only all the best ways."

"I wasn't too hard with you?"

"I wouldn't have it any other way."

"Rory..."

She grasps my forearm. "I'm perfectly fine, Hawken. Look, I can even raise my arm a little more this morning." She lifts her arm until it's even with her shoulder before she winces and drops it back down.

"You'll tell me if I'm ever too rough?"

Her eyes narrow and she twists her mouth. "You say that like you're implying this will happen again?"

Her comment throws me for a loop catching me off guard. I drop my hand from her chin and step back. "Oh. I don't...I didn't...I'm sorry. I thought yo—"

"Don't get your panties in a bunch, Hawken." She grins. "Of course, I want it to happen again. And I'm not just saying that because your dick is better than any toy I've ever owned."

Thank Christ.

"Right." I nod. "Okay, good."

"We should just, you know, set some ground rules."

I turn back to the stove and turn off the burner, my brows furrowing. "Rules? What do you mean?"

"I mean if we're going to be fuck buddies, we should have rules, you know?"

Wait, what?

The small bubble of happiness in my chest deflates at her suggestion.

Fuck buddies?

Who said anything about fuck buddies?

"Wait, I don't understand." I dish out our breakfast and place a plate of eggs and toast in front of her.

"Thanks," she says, grabbing her fork and taking a bite. "Mmm. So good." She swallows before continuing. "Yeah, I gave it a lot of thought before falling asleep last night and it seems like the most logical answer."

"To what?"

"Dex."

"What about Dex?"

"What do you mean, *what about Dex?*" She shovels in another bite. "You know as well as I do, he'll give you hell if he finds out what you've done with his sister."

I'm about to say I don't give a damn what he says, but she continues before I get the chance. "And don't get me started on what he'll say or do with me. So, this way you get the best of both worlds. All the fun sex you want and Dex never has to know."

Scooping a large bite of eggs into my mouth I use my chewing as an excuse to not respond right away, instead playing over all her possible thoughts in my head.

She doesn't want to commit to being with me?

She doesn't want to commit at all?

Last night meant nothing to her?

She didn't like it as much as she said she did?

"And this is what you want?" I finally ask her once I swallow. "Just sex."

She shrugs like we're discussing our favorite brands of

orange juice and not the future of our relationship. "It works, doesn't it? You have a busy schedule..."

Which is almost over for the season.

"I'm busy with school..."

Only for another couple weeks.

"And this way we're not together," she says, using air quotes. "And if we're not together, then there's no breakup. So when this ends, it ends. No hard feelings. And Dex's fragile little heart will be perfectly secure."

There it is.

Her reason for this fucking friends-with-benefits idea.

I'm not even certain she's doing it to save Dex's feelings, but more so to protect her own.

When this ends.

She's already giving us a timeline.

She's afraid of a breakup. She's afraid I don't want her. I watch her across the table silently eating her breakfast and then it hits me.

Every other man in her life has chosen Dex over her.

Dex is my best friend.

In her eyes I'll always choose him over her.

I guess I can see why she would be a little apprehensive and I certainly don't want to accuse her and cause a fight. I'll just have to prove to her she's wrong about me. She's wrong about what I want. And she's wrong about what she wants.

If she needs this for now, I'm willing to play her way.

"Alright. Rules." I nod. "What are your rules?"

She finishes her eggs and sits back, her arms folded over her chest. "Umm, well, I guess no PDA apart from anything we've ever done before."

"So, a hug or a kiss on the cheek is okay?"

"Yeah. When Dex is around you treat me the way you've always treated me."

Like a fantasy I can't have.

Like a dream I never want to wake up from.

Got it.

"What else?"

"Uh, I don't know. I haven't given it that much thought. I guess if you want to see other peo—"

"No other people." I shake my head adamantly, startling her.

Her brows shoot up. "Oh."

"I don't share, Rory. Understand that right now. You're either in or you're out, because if you're in, nobody eats, fucks, or comes close to touching that pussy but me."

She swallows and I expect her to comply, but then she smirks. "What about The Hawk?"

"Fuck me," I whisper with a laugh. Fucking vibrators. I shove my hand through my hair before catching her eye. "If The Hawk gets to be inside you, I get to watch."

She considers my counter offer a minute and then gives me a tiny nod. "Deal."

I release a long sigh. "Okay, so when Dex isn't around?"

"I'm all yours to play with."

"Good." I spring from my chair and grab her by the waist and then toss her over my shoulder.

"Hawk!" She squeals, laughing. "What are you doing?"

"Dex isn't here so you're all mine to play with." I swat her on her ass and she squeals again. "Round four starts now."

"GAME FOUR BABY!" Zeke shouts above the loud music coming from Dex's speaker. Of course, his Taylor Swift playlist is up and running. He's been dancing for the last ten minutes.

The rest of the team hoots and hollers in response to Zeke. We've been pumping ourselves up since we arrived in Boulder this morning for tonight's game. We only need one more win to secure our spot in the Cup Finals. As far as I'm concerned, this game is ours tonight. Now that we're under an hour until gametime, the excitement is on overload. Colby has had two bowls of Lucky Charms so far today, Quinton's wearing the same pair of socks he's worn for every game, not one of us has shaved since the beginning of the playoffs, and of course, Dex refuses to take the ice until he's played through no less than six of his favorite Swift songs.

I, on the other hand, am just stepping out of the shower because for whatever reason, this season, I've gotten into the habit of showering before and after every game. Something about being under the water allows me the opportunity to focus on the job ahead and mentally prepare myself for what to expect on the ice. This time though, all thoughts on tonight's game are out the window. I'm finding it hard to focus on anything other than Rory and our experience in the shower the other night.

I don't bring women into my home. I never have. My penthouse is the one place I know I'm out of public view and free to be me. To do whatever I want without ridicule or judgement. My friends have been there many times, Rory included, but that night with her was different. Not only was it the first time I was intimate with a woman in my home, but it was the first time I've ever fucked in a shower and it was mind numbingly magnificent. Naked and wet Rory now lives rent free in my mind, like a video stuck on repeat and fuck me, if I don't stop thinking about it, I'm going to be forced to walk out of here with a damn chubbie for the entire team to see.

I shut off the water and dry myself off, then slip on my boxer briefs before heading into the dressing room to get into my uniform.

"Whoa! What the fuck is that, Malone?" Quinton asks when I walk into the room. I stop and glance around, not knowing what he's referring to.

"What's what?"

His brows shoot up. "Your back, man."

"What the hell are you talking about?" I try to look over my shoulder but my neck only turns so far.

"Dude." Dex's eyes bulge. "You have huge scratch marks on your back all the way up to your shoulders."

Fuuuuuck.

Rory.

"Uh..."

Think man.

Think really fuckin' fast.

And it better be believable.

"Hawken," Dex laughs. "Did you finally get laid? Because those look a hell of a lot like sex battle scars to me, man. Who was she, huh? Must've been a freak in the sheets for you to have marks like that."

Oh fuck.

If you only knew, Dex.

The guys stare at me with shocked expressions until Quinton coughs, covering his mouth as he turns to hide his face from Dex. I look to some of them for help but each of them busies themselves with their uniform, leaving me completely on my own.

"Uh, yeah. Just some chick I ran into the other night. We'd met before. She was uh, yeah, pretty wild."

God, I can't believe I have to talk about this with him of all people. If he ever knew I was talking about Rory, he would be sick to his stomach.

And then he would castrate me, for sure.

"Good for you, my man!" Dex claps my shoulder. "I know it's been a while. You deserve a little pregame fun."

Please for the love of God stop talking about this.

"Yep."

"You think you'll see her again?"

Absofuckinlutely.

Tonight, when I sneak her into my hotel room.

I give him a quick shrug as I grab my gear and start strapping in. "I don't know. Yeah, maybe."

"Damn right you will. Any woman who leaves her mark like that is a keeper in my book."

The second Dex goes back to belting out the latest Taylor Swift song, I busy myself with getting the rest of my gear on. Milo clears his throat on the other side of me and catches my eye. He doesn't say a word but the conversation between our expressions goes a little something like this:

"Rory?"

"Yep."

"Holy shit, dude."

"I know."

"He still doesn't know?"

"Hell, no."

"You good?"

"So, fucking good. But also, so fucking fucked."

"It'll be alright, man. You'll figure it out."

"Yeah."

I really don't know if it'll be alright though.

Rory holds the cards right now. I've got to play this forbidden game with her if I have any hope of making her my end game.

12

RORY

ME

I need to tell you something. And it's a big something and you're literally the only person I can tell.

SHELLY

Where are you? What did you do? And how much is bail? I've got you, girl.

ME

LOL. No bail needed, but it's very reassuring to know I've got a person to drive the getaway car if I ever need to murder someone.

SHELLY

Absolutely. My minivan makes the best getaway car, I swear. We could drive out to the middle of nowhere and sleep in that sucker. Nobody would find us.

ME

Okay, anyway. I did a thing.

SHELLY

Out with it. Who did you sleep with?

ME

How did you know I slept with someone?

SHELLY

Because if it were anything else, you would've told me by now. And now that I'm thinking about it, if there's a reason you aren't telling Tatum it's because you don't want your brother to know which can only mean one thing. 😏

ME

Shell, he found The Hawk.

y phone rings immediately and I know it's her before I even pick it up.

"Hey."

"WHAAAAT?" she screams on the other end of the line. "YOU'RE KIDDING!"

"Nope. I fucking left it out and he came to my place after the school festival and showered in my bathroom."

"I had to call because you don't want this in writing anywhere, but holy shit, Rory! You slept with him that long ago and you're just NOW telling me?

"No, no, no, no, no." I shake my head even though she can't see me. "But that's kind of where it started. He kissed me that night."

"Hawken Malone kissed you that night? Hawken Malone as in, your brother's best friend?"

"The very same, yes."

"Just so you know I have a nice big glass of wine here so

tell me all the things. Was it good? I bet it was good. God, I need to live vicariously through you right now."

"It was amazing, Shell. It was after their last game. In his shower and then in his bed...several times."

"Several times," she whispers. "Fuck. You're a lucky girl. And oh, my God! They're playing for the Cup! I can't believe they made it to the final round!"

"Right? It's been a whirlwind couple of weeks for them. All the guys are so intense right now. It's like they're in this different kind of focus zone. It's weird, but cool. I've never seen Dex so serious."

"Does that mean you really haven't gotten to see Hawken in a while?"

"Not necessarily. He lives in the building right next door. And between you and me, I think he sees sex as a way to unwind. To rid himself of the pent-up adrenaline at the end of the day."

"Sooo what's the problem here exactly?"

"You know what the problem is."

She chuckles. "Yeah, I get it. He's Dex's friend yadda yadda. Who the hell cares, Ror? You're an adult. He's an adult."

"Mhmm..."

There's a silent pause on the other end and then Shelly speaks again, drawing out each word. "Oooh no. Whaaaat did you do? You did something. That's why you're calling me."

I bite my fingernails because I'm a nervous wreck. "I kind of talked him into a friends-with-benefits situation."

"Becaaaaause...?"

"Uh, because hello? Dex would chop off his balls and

then he would lock me in a room somewhere and I would never see you again."

Shelly laughs. "Oh, I get it. So instead of simply becoming a thing with Hawken Malone, you got him to agree to a friends-with-benefits type of relationship for *my* benefit. So, *we* can still be friends. Do I have that right?"

"Yep. That's about it."

"Uh huh," she says. "You're so full of shit, Rory Foster, but you do you, babe. You soak up as much of that big dick energy as you can."

"Shelly..."

"Yeah?"

"I just couldn't do it."

"Do what?"

"I couldn't tell him I've liked him for years."

"I know, babe."

"What if none of this works out? What if he just sees me as someone to fuck to pass the time? What if he finds someone else and becomes infatuated with her? It would tear me apart."

"Do you want me to tell you that's not going to happen?"

"Yes." I release a heavy sigh. "But no."

"If he's a smart man, Ror, he knows what he's getting himself into. He knows the risks and he's still interested."

"Yeah. I guess."

"So, you're going to enjoy every moment with him. Live your life. Have some fun. In the grand scheme, your brother isn't going to do a damn thing except maybe be a little hurt that the two people he loved most in this life, before Tate and Summer came along, are keeping their feelings from him."

"Aww, that doesn't make me feel better at all, Shell. I just think we should wait until the season is over. He needs to stay focused. They all do."

"Whatever you've got to tell yourself, babe."

"So, you won't tell Tate? I can't tell the WAGS. I don't want this getting back to any of the guys."

"Your secret is safe with me. You know that. You're still the only person who knows Zander was conceived in Jeff's gym storage closet during parent-teacher conferences because he dared me to suck him off."

I blurt out a laugh. "You sucked him off, alright."

Her maniacal laugh lightens my mood. "Damn right. I never turn down a dare, and I'm no pearl-clutching Karen, babe. I'm straight up hoe and you know it."

"I think I want to be you when I grow up."

She outright laughs. "Be careful what you wish for, Rory."

At the sound of the siren every Chicago Red Tails fan is on their feet cheering.

"Oh, my God!" Charlee screams, her hands on her forehead in disbelief. "I can't believe they did it! Two down, and two more to go!"

The Red Tails are currently in the lead two games to one for the championship Cup and the energy in the arena tonight has been off the charts. Game two in our home arena was not our guys' best performance and led to a Milwaukee win. Tonight, however, they look like a completely different team.

"I know! Hawken mentioned something about the guys being pissed the other night because they let Milwaukee through with a win."

"It's true," Carissa says with a nod. "Colby came home so pissed he went downstairs to the gym and worked out for another ninety minutes before he ever spoke to me. And he and Milo played in Milwaukee at one time. They have a ton of respect for those guys."

"Well, they were a different team tonight!" Tatum beams. "Glad I got waxed because he'll be wanting to celebrate tonight."

The girls cackle at Tatum's comment, and I cover my ears and tell her I don't want to hear about my brother.

"Oh, right. Sorry." She laughs and then grasps my arm. "Are you sure you'll be alright tonight? I can tell Dex I'm going to stay with you instead."

"What?" I scoff. "No way. Tonight, I get to order all the room service I want, wear a cushy soft hotel robe, and snuggle in with my book boyfriends until I fall blissfully asleep. Or," I shrug, "I'll just bug Zeke, or Quinton, or Hawken."

Tate's eyes bulge and she gasps. "Oh shit, speaking of Hawken, I don't think I ever told you guys the gossip."

A fleeting panic grows in the bottom of my stomach.

"There's gossip?" Charlee asks.

Carissa rubs her hands together. "Spill the tea, girl. If it's about Hawken, I bet it's good."

Oh God.

"Dex said last week Hawk walked into the locker room after his shower and had scratch marks all down his back."

They all appear a bit confused so I play along with a furrowed brow. "From what? Did he fall or something?"

She shakes her head with a smirk. "Not those kinds of scratch marks."

Carissa gasps, her glance passing to me. "That sly sexy fox. He got himself a possessive piece of ass, huh?"

Oh. My. God.

I whip my head toward her. "Possessive piece of ass? What do you mean?"

"I mean, she marked him. Scratched her huge itch I guess." She smirks. "All down his back."

Yeah, but I didn't do it because I was marking him on purpose.

He's just an amazing lover.

I was in the moment.

Also oh, my God, now Carissa knows!

"Oooh, that's kind of hot." Charlee fans her face.

Yeah, it totally was.

Her eyes narrow. "I wonder if he liked it?"

He didn't say he didn't.

Tatum laughs. "If he's anything like Dex, he probably did. Whoever she was, Dex said Hawk mentioned that he might see her again, sooo." She shrugs. "Maybe we'll be meeting a new friend soon."

See me again.

He's seen me almost every night for the past couple weeks.

Of course, he'll see me again.

"Let's hope we'll be meeting the guys soon," I say, effectively changing the subject. "I'm ready to celebrate."

"Yeah, let's go," Carissa says. "I can get us into the hallway outside their locker room. We can wait for them there."

When we reach the lower level, I notice Colby's brother, Elias standing with his wife outside the locker room. Elias Nelson has worked as the team's accountant for years, so it's no surprise he would travel here for the game. Living in Kentucky now, it's not that far of a drive.

"Hey Elias. Hi Whitney," Carissa greets them both with a hug. "It's so great to see you both."

"We wouldn't miss it," Elias tells her.

"How are the kids?"

Whitney rolls her eyes with a smile. "Goofy with a side of crazy. We're extremely glad our friends were able to watch them for the night so we could get away."

"That's great! Are you guys at the same hotel as the team?"

Elias nods. "Yep. We'll meet everyone there."

"Sounds good!"

At that moment, the guys finally start to file out of the locker room, freshly showered and dressed in their suits. It's chaos in the hallway as everyone celebrates their win with cheers, high fives, hugs, and kisses. Quinton lifts me off my feet in a bear hug as I squeal in celebration with him and Zeke gives me a sweet hug as well. Dex is all over Tatum, Charlee is kissing Milo, and Carissa and Colby are now chatting with his brother and Whitney. That leaves the last pair of eyes to meet mine among the small crowd.

His stare is intense but happy and because it's what we

would usually do, I have no problem jumping into a hug with Hawken.

"Congratulations Hawk," I murmur when I wrap my arms around his neck in a tight embrace. His duffle bag on his back, he wraps both arms around me nearly taking my breath away.

"Thanks," he says, and then moves his lips closer to my ear. "Do I get to pick my reward?"

"Hmm, what did you have in mind?"

"I have some ideas," he whispers. "And they all include the sweetest pussy I've ever eaten."

"Well, I guess that counts me out as I've eaten nothing but a diet of onion rings and garlic fries for the past two days." I lift my shoulder in a teasing shrug. "Oh well. Your loss, big guy."

Hawk throws his head back in laughter as he lowers me to my feet and then wraps an arm around my neck. "No worries sweetheart. I'll order all the pineapple room service has to offer."

The guys don't stay in the hotel restaurant long, nor did any of them indulge in an alcoholic beverage tonight, each of them choosing water, iced tea, or soda instead. I'm impressed. I've never seen them act like such a tight group of focused athletes before and it almost makes me wonder if Hawken is going to want me with him tonight or if it might be better for me to sleep in my own room. I don't want to be the cause of his head not being in the right place.

I'm just finishing up brushing my teeth when my phone dings.

HAWKEN

Heeeere kitty, kitty, kitty...

ME

gasp LOL! Is this your attempt at a booty call?

HAWKEN

More like a pussy call. Is it working?

ME

Hmm, you know, I don't think it is just yet. Better try harder.

HAWKEN

I've only got one towel here so you choose. Will it dry your eyes or dry your thighs?

ME

LOL. Definitely getting better...

HAWKEN

How about you get your pretty little self down here and spread your legs for me so I can spend the next hour sliding my tongue through my sweet reward and then fuck you as many times as I can until we both pass out.

I don't even tell him I'm on my way, but less than two minutes later I'm lightly tapping on his door. He swings it open, his brows lifting as if to ask me if the coast is clear. I nod and he beams, wrapping an arm around me and lifting me into his room, the door closing behind us.

"Fuck, I've missed you." Those are the only words he

gets out before his mouth collides with mine, his insatiable need palpable as he tugs on my thighs until my legs are wrapped around his waist. He carries me blindly toward the bed, his hands firmly digging into my ass, rubbing, kneading.

Holy hell, it's a turn on I didn't see coming.

"Your scent...fuck it's..." He inhales a deep breath at my neck as he peppers kisses up and down my skin. "You're intoxicating."

A slight giggle escapes my lips. "Maybe you should be wearing my jersey then, huh? Thanks again by the way for having this cleaned. It's perfect and smells more like you than me, in my opinion."

"You're welcome. Anything for you. And I'm pretty damn sure I'll be wearing you soon enough."

He lays me down on the bed and then tucks his fingers into my spandex shorts and panties, pulling them off in one smooth movement.

Whoa.

"Impatient, are we?" I tease. He responds with his strong hands sliding up my inner thighs, pushing them apart. His head dips down and his warm tongue slides through me, circling over my sensitive skin.

"I'm a man who knows what he wants, Rory," he growls. "And I've been dying to eat you all fucking day. I'm going to need you to give me a minute...or twenty, while I take what's mine."

My back arches off the bed at the merciless stroke of his tongue against my body.

"Oooh God, Hawk..."

"I know, Baby," he croons. "But I can't get enough.

Need more..." His hands on my hips, he pulls me tighter against him, a gapless connection between his mouth and my flesh. His tongue dips inside me, swirling, sucking, taking. "Want more."

He moans against my skin and it's like a deep throbbing vibrator. "Shit, Hawken I—"

Knock, Knock, Knock.

My eyes bulge and I freeze when someone knocks on Hawken's door, but it's like he doesn't even hear it and continues with his sensual assault, two of his fingers sliding inside me.

My eyes roll back in my head and I moan. "Hawken!"

Knock, knock, knock.

"Dude, it's me. Open up."

My thighs have never snapped together so fast, locking Hawken's face between them.

"HAWKEN!" I whisper shout. "IT'S MY FUCKING BROTHER!"

He chuckles and separates my legs enough to release his head. "He'll go away."

"No, he won't. It's Dex. You know he's not going away."

Knock, knock, knock.

"Hawk!"

I squirm out of his grasp and off the bed. "I have to hide!"

"Ooor we could just let him walk in and figure it out."

"Are you kidding me right now? You're about to play for the Cup! You really want to do this to him right fucking now?"

He rubs the back of his neck. "Alright then, what do you suggest?"

I gesture to the door. "Tell him you're coming."

"Coming!" he shouts, tossing his arms up in an over-stated shrug and a helpless smile. It's not like it takes that many steps for a man his stature to get to the door. This is getting more awkward by the second.

I turn in a circle looking for the best place to hide but nothing makes sense. Can't go under the bed. The closet doesn't have a door so that's out.

"Fuck!"

"Bathroom," he whispers, gesturing with his head. "Shower?"

"Yes! Okay!"

Grabbing my shorts and panties, I run into the bath-room and jump in the shower, pulling the curtain closed and praying to every holy being out there that Dex doesn't find me in here.

Because explaining what I'm doing in Hawken Malone's bathtub will be next to impossible.

13

HAWKEN

I don't know why I'm finding this so comical when I should probably be freaking out, but I finally open my hotel room door to find Dex standing there with a puzzled look on his face.

"What are you doing here?"

He walks into my room like he owns the place, turning his head to the left and then the right.

"Do you have someone here with you?"

Fuck.

"No."

"I thought I heard voices."

"Voices?"

"Yeah." He laughs. "Voices."

He steps near the bathroom and my heart rate rises. "Well, that's because I was tongue fucking your sister, man. Can't you see you're interrupting?"

He spins around, giving me the goofiest smile I think I've ever seen and it takes everything in my control to keep a straight face.

"Oh, so she's the mystery girl scratching up your back. Is that what you're trying to tell me?"

Hmm. Could this be that easy?

I fold my arms across my chest and raise an eyebrow. "What if she is? What are you going to do about it?"

Dex cackles and then flips me off in response. "First of all, fuck you, asshat. If she ever heard you talking this way about her, she would pulverize your nuts and sprinkle them on top of her next batch of peach cobbler and secondly, you know how I know you're lying?"

"I'm sure you're going to tell me."

"Rory teaches kindergarten for a fucking living, man. She wouldn't hurt a goddamn fly, let alone mark a man. Especially you."

"Oh yeah? Why not me?"

"Why are we even talking about this?"

"I don't know Dex." I finally let out a laugh. "Because you're still talking. What are you doing here anyway? Speaking of tongue fucking, I have yet to hear Tatum screaming down the hallway."

"Oh, her brothers traveled to the game. She's downstairs saying goodbye to them and I was bored. Knew you were alone, so, you know...I've got to piss."

"So, you just came here to use my bathroom?"

"No," he chuckles as I hear him lift the lid of the toilet. "But piss waits for no man."

I roll my eyes and bring a palm to my forehead, holding my breath as he relieves himself with the door wide open... and his sister standing in the tub next to him.

I sit on my bed and cringe.

I'm sorry Rory.

I'm really sorry, Rory.

Like, super fucking sorry.

I'll owe you big time for this.

"Two more to go baby!" Dex shouts from the bathroom. "That Cup will be ours."

He flushes and then I hear the sink running.

"Damn right it is. It'll sure make Key West even more fun this year, huh?"

"Oh, hell yeah. Tate's been so tired lately with all the end of the year shit plus Summer. It'll be amazing to have her there with no kids for the week." He scoffs out a laugh. "Not that I don't love my baby girl, but it's been a while since we've had a good night of fucking without a kid waking up throughout the night. I might never let her leave the room. I might just hang out with my dick inside her all fucking week if she'll let me."

I inwardly cringe once again knowing Rory is in my bathroom hearing every word.

"You gonna invite the girl?" He glances at me.

"The girl?"

"Your back scratcher," he says, almost annoyed that I'm not following him. "You said you might see her again. She had to have been a good lay, man. You've had more pep in your step in the last few weeks than I've seen in a long time."

"Have I?"

"You know you can tell me about her, right?"

"Your sister? Dude, you already know her."

He laughs again. "Fuckin' asshole."

If only I could really tell him.

"You know, I think it's just that it's new. So, I'm not

sure if it's going to be a thing or not. Right now, we're just having fun when we can."

"I get it." He smirks. "A little pussy testing never hurt anyone. I'm happy for you, Hawk."

"Thanks, man."

God, I've got to get him out of this room.

For Rory's sake.

I clear my throat and swallow back my pride. He'll believe me in a heartbeat. "You know before you showed up, I was watching porn...hence the voices you heard."

He looks at the powered off television and then slowly turns back to me, a lazy smile spreading across his mouth.

"Right. Of course, you were. That makes perfect sense." He hops up and heads for the door. "Sorry, man. Pretend I was never here."

I laugh. "That's really hard to do when you're standing in the middle of my hotel room, asshole."

He waves his hand, dismissing me. "I was never here. I'm leaving. Enjoy bro."

I call after him. "Night."

As soon as the door clicks behind him, I spring off my bed and leap into the bathroom, pulling back the shower curtain. There Rory sits with her knees pulled up against her chest, her hands over her ears and her eyes squeezed shut. I have to laugh. She's fucking adorable.

I tap her knee and her eyes spring open. "Is he gone?"

"Yep."

"He fucking peed in here, Hawken!"

I throw my head back in laughter. "I'm so sorry you had to be a witness to it."

"I mean it's not like I haven't heard him pee before, but

it's been probably twenty years since he's peed literally in my presence."

Still laughing, I reach down and help her up. "Oh shit, I'm sorry, Ror. I felt bad at the time, but now it's just damn funny."

Once she's out of the tub she slaps me on the arm. "And you seriously told him you were tongue fucking me?"

"I wasn't lying, was I?"

"Oh, my God! You're impossible. And porn? Really?"

"Absolutely, porn. I'm a genius, Rory. Believe me."

"Uh, I think the jury is still out on that one."

"Porn is always the easiest excuse. Especially with your brother. He'll always believe me and he'll always leave me alone. Especially now that he's committed to someone. He probably assumes I'm a single sad sap."

"You mean watching porn isn't a team sport?"

"Fuck no. We jack off on our own, thank you very much."

Her eyes turn almost catlike when she stops and catches my eye. "Is that so?"

"Mhmm."

She places herself directly in front of me, dragging her hand down my chest until she reaches the elastic waistband of my shorts. Then she dips her hand inside and cups my balls.

Mother fuuuuuck.

"And when was the last time you jacked off all by yourself, Mr. Malone?"

"Last week when you couldn't spend the night with me. I took a shower and pictured you, Lady Bug," I confess with a guttural groan. "Sprawled out on that magnificent yellow chair of yours...wet and willing for me." She squeezes my now growing cock in her hand, causing me to hiss through my teeth.

"Go on," she prods, a challenging glint in her eye.

Walking her backwards, I take the hem of her jersey and lift it off her body. "And then I thought about how good it felt that night in my shower, when my stiff cock was fucking this pretty little mouth of yours," I tell her, smoothing my thumb over her bottom lip. She nips at it playfully with her teeth. "God, you give the best head I've ever had."

"Hmm." She smiles with a look of satisfaction and runs her fingertips up my shaft. "Keep going."

"And then I soaped up my fist and squeezed my cock the way your pussy squeezes me after I've made you come. Like you're milking me, like you're taking every last drop of my cum like the greedy girl I know you are."

She licks her lips as she yanks down my shorts and underwear. "If I'm greedy, it's because you've made me this way, Hawken."

"Sorry not sorry, sweetheart."

We finally make it to the bed and she lays down, my cock still in her hand. She brings her legs up and opens them wide for me. "No need to apologize. The time for talking is over. I need your cock inside me."

Crawling onto the bed, hovering over her, I settle myself between her legs and line myself up with her entrance. "It would be my greatest pleasure."

The timer on my oven goes off just as I finish cutting and plating the brownies I made this morning. Grabbing the oven mitts, I open the oven door and pull out the cookie sheet of freshly made chocolate chip cookies.

Rory's favorite.

I place the sheet on a cooling rack and then clean up the rest of my mess in the kitchen, checking my watch when I finish.

"One hour to go," I tell myself.

I've had this day marked on my calendar in my phone since Rory's school year started. Maybe she doesn't realize it, but every single year that I've known her, she's come home sad and depressed that her school year is over. Not because she doesn't relish the relaxation of summer break but more because she's sad to see her students leave her classroom. She does such a wonderful job pouring herself into her classroom and the needs of her students. The bonds she creates are unbelievable. I could tell that simply from seeing how the older kids still cling to her. They all love her, and she loves each of them uniquely. I suppose it's a bit of a downer when she has to say goodbye to all the students she's loved all year.

In past years, I would be hanging out with Dex watching hockey finals as we were not always playing in them. I would be there, in her home when she would walk in and cry for hours before her brother would do or say something to make her laugh. I used to give her a hug and try to tell her a joke to make her smile, but inside, my heart hurt for her. I understand the letdown. The bittersweet feeling of saying goodbye.

This year, I have a plan.

Her feelings are hers and I'll encourage her to feel them as much or as little as she wants, but I've been working on a plan all day to hopefully make her feel loved and hopefully bring a bit of fun and happiness to the end of her year. There's a chance she'll see this all as a little too romantic for the arrangement we have, but at some point, I have to get Rory to see I want more than just a physical relationship with her.

I can only hope my plan will help.

At half past four, I'm standing outside her penthouse knowing damn well what I'm about to come face to face with when she answers the door.

And I'm right.

The door slowly opens and there she is.

Comfy shorts and an off the shoulder t-shirt.

Hair in a messy bun.

Black rimmed glasses over her blood shot, teary eyes.

Feet in a pair of pink Crocs.

She's the most beautiful girl I've ever seen and I can't help but smile at her even though she doesn't return the emotion.

"Hey," she says. "I'm sorry, Hawk. I should've texted earlier."

"You okay?"

She nods, but her tears say otherwise. "I'll be fine. Saying goodbye is just..."

"Fucking hard," I say for her. More tears spill down her soft cheeks as she wipes her nose.

"Yeah. Anyway, I'm not much company. I'm sorry."

My brows pinch when I frown, stepping inside and lifting her chin. "Hey. First of all, you're never bad company Rory. No matter what condition you're in. And secondly, that's why I'm here."

"Huh?"

"I know your last day with your kids is hard on you. I know saying goodbye sucks even if you'll see them again in a few months. They're forever your babies. Your little humans whose minds you helped shape. You love them."

She sniffles. "I do. So much."

"Come here." I pull her toward me and wrap her in a comforting hug. She sinks against me, sniffling lightly, allowing me to run my hands through her hair. "I have no doubt in my mind those kids felt your love all year and I know from witnessing it myself how much they continue to love you even as they move from one class to the next each year. You're a fantastic teacher, Rory. Don't ever forget that."

"Thank you, Hawk."

"Now, I need you to grab your keys because you're coming with me."

"I am?" She sniffles again.

"Mhmm. I have something planned that will hopefully have you ending your night with a smile."

"Are we going out somewhere?"

I shake my head. "Fuck no. Big game tomorrow. The last thing I need to do is be seen in public. Plus, I knew you would appreciate a quiet night at home."

Her shoulders fall and I'm surprised by just how much stress she was holding on to.

"A quiet night at home is perfect. Is it okay if I look like this?"

I don't even have to give her a once over to be able to

answer her question. "You're perfect, Rory. Just the way you are."

"But—"

"And before you say but what if you get cold because apparently my place is an ice box compared to yours, you know I have plenty of things you can wear to keep you warm."

Her eyes brighten a bit and she starts to smile. "Like those sweatpants I love so much?"

"Yeah." I chuckle knowing how goddamn adorable she looks wearing my clothes, which are several sizes too big for her but she doesn't care. "And my hoodie is waiting for you too. I promise a night of snuggles and chocolate."

"Oh, my God, I think you just described my Heaven." She grabs her keys off the hook by the door. "I'm ready. Let's go."

Because she's literally in the building next to mine, we walk to my place and then take the elevator to the top floor. The moment I open my door, her jaw drops and she gasps.

"Ooooh, my God, Hawken. What did...how...this is... beautiful."

In the middle of my living room there are sheets hanging from hooks in my ceiling. They surround a plush white area rug that's nestled on the floor just inside the perimeter of my sectional couch. Several oversized pillows line the edges of the couch fortifying the walls of this home-made living room fort. Strewn about the rug are more fuzzy blankets than any one person needs to own, and the piece de resistance? Small white lights lining the sheets give the room the perfect romantic ambiance.

"You like it?"

"Like it?" Her hand is on her chest as she walks through the room gazing at our snuggle pad for the evening. "I think I'm in love." She turns back toward me. "You did all this? For me?"

"Not just this. There's more."

"Hawken, this is…"

Aaaand cue more tears.

"This might be the nicest thing anyone has ever done for me."

"That can't possibly be true."

She steps up and throws her arms around my neck. "Thank you for this, Hawk. I really do love it."

"You're welcome, Ror." I wrap my arms around her and breathe her in for a few quick moments before releasing her and gesturing down the hall. "Now go put your sweats on and get comfortable while I prepare all the snacks and your chocolate milk. Then it's you, me, our fort, and all the romcoms you can handle tonight."

Her face lights up in my direction. "Best. Night. Ever." She kisses my cheek and practically runs down the hallway to my room.

I call after her, "No. Best night ever is when you take off your bra so I can feel you up in the middle of the movie!"

"I'm not even wearing a bra!" she shouts from my room.

"Jesus Christ don't tell me that," I mutter to myself, amused, as I grab the prepared charcuterie boards. One is covered in several types of crackers and cheese with a garnish of grapes, while the other consists of homemade chocolate chip cookies, brownies, pretzels, milk duds, and chocolate kisses.

When Rory finally comes back out to the living room, she looks remarkably cute in my sweatpants rolled at her hips and around her ankles, and my oversized hoodie, sans bra of course. I pat the spot next to me.

"Come here. Join me."

With an eager smile, she climbs into the space and crawls over to where I'm sitting against several pillows and maneuvers herself right next to me, my arm around her pulling her close.

"You smell good," she comments as she brings the neck of the hoodie she's wearing to her nose and inhales.

"I'm glad you like it." I pull a grape from the snack board in front of us and feed one to her.

"Mmm and he feeds me grapes? A girl could get used to this, you know?"

"If it meant you looking this delightfully charming and snuggling with me like this all the time, I'd feed you grapes every damn day, Rory."

She giggles. "You like me in your clothes?"

Like you?

I fuckin' love you in my clothes.

"Uh, yeah, Ror. It's a turn on."

"No funny business," she declares, pointing her finger at me. "You promised snuggles and romcoms."

I pull her into me as tightly as I can get her and she leans her head back on my shoulder. "No funny business. I swear. Just snuggles and snacks and if you want it later, take out from wherever you want."

In reality, this is the perfect night for me too as much as it is for her. Hell, it's enough just to have her here with me in my space. I no longer sleep well on the nights we're apart. Over the past several years, and certainly the past few months, Rory has become an integral part of my life.

I enjoy being around her.

I feed off her goofiness.

But she also calms me.

I'm at peace when she's around.

I'm falling for her.

I'm falling for my best friend's sister.

And at some point, I'm going to need the entire world to know it.

14

RORY

"Hawken." My voice is both hoarse and breathless as I reach down and push my fingers through his hair. My body writhing of its own accord against his lustful tongue. This is unlike any wakeup call I've ever had. He doesn't answer me at first. He continues to lazily stroke his tongue through me, licking, sucking, tasting me, and my body has definitely woken up and taken notice.

"I had no idea you offered wakeup calls like this. Ooooh God, Yessss."

He's so painstakingly slow in his assault and my body responds with a sudden flush of warmth and a tingling pleasure.

"Good morning, Lady Bug." He smiles against my skin as he peppers kisses up my abdomen, pushing my shirt up little bits at a time until my breasts are bared to him. "God, you are the most beautiful woman I have ever seen." Fondling one of my breasts in his warm palm, he lowers his head and feathers his tongue over my hardened peaks.

I arch my back in response, feeling my whole body stretch as it wakes up with the help of Hawken's expert pampering. "How long have you been awake?"

He moans against me. "Long enough to decide I didn't want to get out of bed until I woke you properly."

He switches to my other breast, my lower extremities now throbbing for more of his touch.

"Hawke..." His name is a moan and a cry at the same time. He raises his head to look at me, smiling as he hovers over me.

"Do you miss me, Lady Bug?"

"You know I do." I boldly take the lead and slide his hand down between my legs. He leans down to kiss me but his lips only barely touch mine as he breathes me in while dragging his finger through my arousal, circling my clit.

"Fuuuuuck, Rory. So wet and ready."

My heart rate quickens as I concentrate on the pleasure, he brings my body.

"Yes, Hawk. Please."

"You're ready for me?"

"Yes." I lift my hips to meet his hand, urging him to do more. Give me more. I need more. "Don't make me beg."

"I wouldn't dream of it."

He slides off the bed for a quick moment to remove his boxer briefs, freeing his cock and palming it in his hand.

God, it's incredibly sexy to see him handling himself.

Crawling back onto his king-sized bed, he maneuvers between my legs and lines himself up at my entrance. With tender ease, he pushes inside me, first the tip and then inch by delicious inch until he's in as far as he can go.

"Shit, Rory. It's amazing every fucking time."

My eyes closed and my head back, I revel in the satis-fying feeling of fullness. "It so is."

"Look at me, Ror. Watch me take you."

My eyes spring open and I lift onto my elbows to watch our connection—holy fuck why has nobody ever told me sex is so much more pleasurable when you watch your partner?

"You take me in so damn perfectly, Ror. God, so fucking tight. Fucking perfect."

"Hawken, oh, God, you ne—"

My phone rings on the nightstand next to me. A familiar Taylor Swift song. A ringtone that can only be set for one person.

"Shit!" I squeeze my eyes closed. "It's my brother."

"Let it go," he tells me as he moves his body against mine, pulling out and thrusting back in. I cry out when his cock collides with the perfect spot inside me. Holy shit I think I might just have an out of body experience.

"Oh, my God, Hawk! Don't stop. Right fucking there!"

My phone silences and then begins to ring again but at this point, I'm so fucking close to an orgasm I couldn't answer the phone if I tried.

"What does he want?" Hawken asks me.

The same question drives through my head until finally it hits me. "Fuck! We're supposed to meet for breakfast."

Hawken glances down to our connection, slowing his pace, and then meets my gaze with a mischievous glint in his eye. "Answer it."

"What?"

"You heard me."

"You are NOT serious right now."

He pulls his cock out of me, rubbing my arousal up and down his shaft. "Answer it or you don't get this cock."

My jaw dops. "Oh my...you're really serious?"

He expects me to talk to my brother while he fucks me?

Ummm...earth to Rory. That's fucking hot.

What your brother doesn't know won't hurt him.

Live a little.

Take a risk!

Do it!

Licking my lips, I reach for my phone and swipe to answer Dex's call.

"Hey."

"What took you so long? You okay?"

"Okay? Yeah. I'm fine, why?"

Hawken lines himself back in and thrusts inside me so hard I'm pretty sure I see stars. I gasp. Wasn't expecting that at all.

"What's wrong?"

His cock feels so good my eyes nearly roll right out of my head.

"Ooohhhuuuuh, nothing. I was just umm...watching this cat video."

He thrusts into me at a steadied pace and then presses his thumb against my clit and I have to bite my lip not to cry out.

"So, breakfast?"

"Mhmm." That's all I can say.

"You still want to go? I need to get my protein in before practice."

Now Hawken's hands are on my breasts, his fingers

pinching my nipples as he silently drives into me over, and over, and over again.

"YES!" I scream and then clear my throat much to Hawken's amusement. "I mean yes. He's in."

Fuck.

"I mean I'm...I'm in. Yeah. Wherever you want to go."

"Great. How about Jerry's Diner in about twenty?"

Hawken shakes his head, bending down to pull my nipple into his mouth as his thrusts pick up in speed and intensity.

"Shiiit. Uh, better make it thirty."

Dex laughs. "Are you taking a shit right now? What are you doing?"

"Dripping."

God, did I say that the way I think I said it?

"What?"

"Spilled my coffee. It's dripping. That's all. No big deal. I just need to get it all cleaned up."

"Alright. Jerry's in thirty?"

"Jerry's in thirty."

"Need me to pick you up?"

"Nooooooo, I'm good. I'll uh, I'll meet you there."

"Alright, weirdo. See you then."

"Okay. Bye!"

I don't even look to make sure the call is disconnected before I chuck my phone across the room and throw my head back in pure carnal lust for the man giving me all his big dick energy this morning.

"HAWKEN!" I scream. "Fucking Christ, I need to come, Hawk! Oh, my God!"

"Me too, Babe. Fuck, you make me so damn hard and you feel incredible."

I slide my hand between our bodies, rubbing my clit with my finger while Hawken thrusts into me, grabbing my breasts as he does so. Squeezing, kneading, fondling.

"Haaaaawk!" I lift my legs so they're almost on his shoulders changing where his cock hits me and that's all it takes to light the spark inside my body that makes me explode.

I clutch his cock from the inside, his eyes rolling back as he gasps and leans forward over me, holding himself up on his forearms. "Touch me, Rory. Fucking touch me," he begs, his forehead resting at the crook of my neck. I fold my arms over his back and dig in with my nails, marking him again as he nears his climax. The groan emanating from him at my touch is louder than I've ever heard before.

"Son of a fuuuuuck! Shit. I'm coming. Oh, fuck, Roooory!" Hawken's orgasm hits him hard as he slams into me, and for the first time he calls my name when he comes.

Holy shit.

He. Came. Saying. My. Name.

And his voice...

Guttural, yet satisfied.

Tormented, but loving.

And it's in this moment I realize, I love hearing him say my name.

Hawken pants hard against my chest. "Rory."

There it is again.

The way he says my name. This time a sigh of relief.

A sigh of satisfaction.

A sigh of peace.

Gah! It gives me butterflies.

"You know, I think you've ruined me for all women."

I drag my nails, lightly this time, around his back in calming circles. "Sorry not sorry."

He rolls to the side, relieving me of his weight, but pulls me with him so we're both facing each other. He places a gentle kiss on my forehead and then my nose and my lips.

"You're an amazing woman, Rory Foster."

I huff out a soft laugh. "I think you're just saying that because you're drunk on sex."

He grins. "I think you're right. Hello. My name is Hawken Malone and I'm a pussy addict." He shakes his head, smiling when I snort in laughter. "And I'm not even sorry about it."

I don't know what makes me do it, but I roll toward him enough that he lifts me on top of him. "Well as long as it's my pussy you're drunk on and not some other bimbo's..."

His smile falls and he brushes my sex-crazed hair from my face. "As far as I'm concerned other women don't exist anymore. Only you."

Pretending to brush something off his chest, I glance down, shaking my head. "Don't say that. One day you'll be tired of me and you'll want someone else."

He doesn't respond right away and I wonder if he's fallen asleep, but when I finally raise my gaze, he's staring at me. Eyes wide, like he can see into my very soul. His mouth opens like he's going to say something but then closes, his brows furrowed.

His mouth opens again. "Is that what you thi—"

Taylor Swift plays loud and clear—on his phone this time, and as much as I want to laugh that my brother is now calling him, Hawken isn't laughing. His jaw tenses and he huffs in frustration.

Cringing, I tell him, "You may as well answer him. You know he'll keep trying until you do."

I sit up so I'm straddling him and watch as he picks up his phone and accepts his call.

"S'up Asshat? Yep...nope...yep. Yeah, I can do that... Nah, I'll grab her. Yeah, no worries. See you soon."

He lays his phone down on the bed beside him and runs his hands up my thighs. "Looks like I'm coming to breakfast with you."

"Of course, he would call you too. I should've just asked him if I should bring you along."

"He just wants to make sure I eat a shit ton of carbs and protein before tonight."

"Alright, I just need to shower quickly and I can be ready to go. As long as you don't mind my looking like a troll."

"I love trolls," he says with a smirk. He sits up and wraps his arms around me, causing me to squeal but then his face is serious again. "But can we go back to what you said for a minute? Because I meant what I said about not wanting other women, Ror. I think we should talk abou—"

I cut him off with a kiss. I even use tongue so he knows I'm being sincere, but my nerves are getting the better of me right now and I'm scared as hell to have any kind of conversation about what Hawken and I are really doing together.

"I know, but can we talk about it later? Today is a massive day for you. I don't want anything on your mind for the rest of this day except hockey. Playing hockey and winning hockey." I take his face in my hands. "Tonight is the night, Hawken. You guys are going to win this, I can feel it."

"Yeah. We can wait. As long as you promise to be next to me in this bed tonight no matter the outcome." He goes in for a kiss right behind my ear and happiness blooms inside me.

"I'll be here."

"Good. Let's shower."

He carries me into his shower where we quickly wash ourselves and then dry off and get dressed. When I finally make it out to the living room, he's waiting for me with a proud smile on his face.

"Oh, my God! You did not!" I laugh at the t-shirt he's wearing.

"Oh, I so did," he answers. "You like it?"

Standing at the door like the newest bouncer at a club, Hawken sports a brand-new black t-shirt with white lettering that spells out, THE HAWK across the chest.

All I can do is shake my head. "I can't wait for you to explain this to Dex."

15

HAWKEN

"Hawken, congratulations on getting this far, it must be an amazing feeling knowing the team has not only clenched each level of the play-offs up to now, but you're about to play game five of the Cup finals and could potentially win it all here tonight."

Several microphones and cellphones are pointed toward me awaiting my response.

"For sure, it feels remarkable. We've worked our asses off this entire season to get where we are today, but there is still a game to be played which means there's still work to do, eh?"

"How important does this game become knowing you've won eleven games of these playoffs but still have one if not a possible two games to go."

"Well first of all," I smile at Nicholas Berti, sports reporter for the National Sports Broadcasting Network, "let's not talk about a possible two games, eh?" I raise my pointer finger. "We'll be taking this game tonight. You want to know how important it is, it's everything. We're leaving it all out on the ice tonight, and the way we've been playing with the amount of focus we've had these last couple games, I have no doubt we'll be celebrating when that final bell rings."

"Do you feel a sense of responsibility to help keep the focus throughout the team, knowing that for the younger guys in this room, it's their first time ever getting to play in the playoffs?"

"Sure." I shrug. "I mean we all have a responsibility. Some of us who have been in the league for years now have known what's coming and how to prepare for it. From there we have to trust each other and play the game harder than we've ever played and we're going to do that tonight."

Nicholas nods. "Thanks so much Hawken and good luck tonight."

"Thanks."

I step out of the press room and head down the hall to the locker room so I can get out of this suit and spend a few minutes on the bike to warm up my legs. Dex already has his Taylor Swift playlist up and running while he's in the shower. Milo and Quinton are taping their sticks.

"Hey man, how was the interview?" Quinton asks.

"I hate interviews," I state, pulling off my suit jacket and unbuttoning my dress shirt.

He snorts. "Right? Some of those people ask the dumbest questions."

"Yeah, I get it. It's their jobs and all, but sometimes it would be nice to be asked something creative and not 'hey how important do you think tonight is?'"

Milo laughs. "Is that what they asked you?"

"Yep." I pull my dress shirt off and strip out of my dress pants, exchanging them for my workout shorts.

"Where's Miller?" I ask the guys.

"Goalie warmup," Milo answers. "Nelson's around here somewhere. I think I saw him in the gym earlier."

"Good, I'm heading there now for a quick leg warmup." I bend over to tie my tennis shoes and the moment I stand up, Milo and Quinton are both grinning at me.

"What?"

Milo turns his head to make sure nobody is coming and then gestures with his chin. "Looks like you had another good night with a she who has a proclivity for scratching."

Quinton chuckles and I wipe a hand down my face.

"Shit. I guess I need a t-shirt, eh?"

Milo nods his head. "If you don't want questions from her brother, then yes."

I backtrack to my locker and pull out a muscle shirt and slide it over my head. "Tonight, is not the night for more questions."

"Sooo this is getting serious, no?"

Running a hand through my hair, I release a sigh. "I don't know."

"Well, it's easy to figure out. If she's the one marking you like that, things must be pretty damn good."

"Yeah, I mean..." I check for Dex again but still hear him in the shower singing away with his BFF Taylor. Still, I lower my voice just in case. "That part is...fucking amazing. I'm not going to lie."

Milo stops his taping and studies me. "Buuut?"

"She thinks this is a friends-with-benefits situation."

"And that's not what you think?"

I plop myself down on the bench in front of them. "I mean, don't get me wrong, she's the perfect girl, eh? She's sweet, compassionate, funny, she loves hockey but doesn't take any of our shit. She's great at so many things. She has the most likeable personality and she's drop dead gorgeous."

"Then what's the problem? You afraid of Dex?"

"I don't know." I shake my head. "I really can't read him sometimes. I have no idea how he would feel about me making things official with her, and right now, I get the impression she doesn't want that either. Or she does want it, but she's too afraid to take the leap because she thinks I'll get bored with her and won't want her anymore."

Quinton frowns. "Rory thinks that? Really?"

"Yeah. It's crazy to me. She's scared. So, I went along with this friends-with-benefits thing because one, I've had a crush on her for years and two, I can't stand the thought of her with another guy."

"So, what are you going to do?"

"She wants to wait until the playoffs are over to think about anything else. To tell Dex, I guess. She wants us to stay focused on what's important."

"She's not wrong there, you know?" Milo states.

"I know." Another heavy sigh escapes me.

"Dex won't like it if there's even a chance you two might break up."

"I have no intention of that ever happening."

Milo's eyes grow wide, as does the grin on his face. "You really like her?"

Without a doubt, I nod. "I think I might love her."

Quinton chuckles. "You alright having Dex as your brother-in-law?"

I stand with a laugh. "Fuck. We may as well be. We're basically family now anyway."

"You want my advice or just an ear?" Milo offers.

"Advice if you have it."

"If you love her, then respect her wishes. Wait until after the playoffs and then tell her how you feel. Make her see you mean it. I have a feeling things will go your way."

"Hold on for one more day," Quinton sings, much to our amusement.

"Dumbass." I fist bump him as I head for the door. "Thanks guys. I think I needed to get that off my chest."

"Get what off your chest?" Dex asks coming around the corner wrapped in his towel.

Milo winks and answers, "He was just telling us about La Roi's pregame interview. Talking shit about us like usual."

"Meh, that asshat likes to stir the shit pot. That's all. We've got this." He glances at me in the doorway. "You warming up?"

"Yep."

"Twenty minutes. Then it's dance party time. Everyone's in tonight."

I huff out an amused laugh. "Yes, Sir. Consider this my official RSVP."

"This is it, Gentlemen," Colby announces before we step out of the tunnel and onto the ice. He's forced to shout because of the pregame music and the roar of tonight's home crowd. "We leave it all on the ice tonight and that cup will be in our hands. Tonight, we push ourselves. We give this game everything we've got. We show Milwaukee we came not just to play, but to fucking win. No regrets when that final bell rings."

The team cheers with our fearless captain as he puts his hand in the middle of our circle. "On three, gentlemen. One...two...three."

"HUSTLE, HIT, AND NEVER QUIT!"

Game faces on, we wait for the announcer to call us to the ice and then the showdown begins.

We make it through the first and second periods with each team scoring two goals apiece for a tied score of four to four. Milwaukee brought their A-game tonight as much as we did and they're definitely making us work for this win. After a blank third period, we're forced into overtime for a sudden death twenty-minute play until one of us scores the game winning goal.

Landric faces off with Michlen and the puck flies to me. I try to get it to Shay but it's turned over by Milwaukee's La Roi and taken down the ice. He slaps the puck into Zeke's territory and my ass puckers at the thought that we could lose this game right here right now. Zeke blocks La Roi's attempt and Nelson is out in front to take possession.

"Thank fuck," I say to nobody but myself as I race to accept Nelson's pass to me. Dex is right with me and I give the puck a fake shot to Milwaukee's net as Dex takes control. He circles the track but he'll wind one off the stick and the puck becomes available. Shay tries for the shot but Brewster makes the block and I see my opportunity the moment it comes. I'm there for the rebound, slapping it into the net right behind Brewster and SCOOOOOORE!

The crowd is on their feet in a sea of red as the goal siren blares around the arena.

"FUUUUUUUUUCK YEAAAAH!" Dex gets to me first and practically picks me up in a bear hug and we're soon accompanied by the entire team. I don't feel the ice between my feet for several long minutes and when I finally do, we're all against the glass where the WAGS and other fans are jumping and shouting and slapping the glass from the other side in celebration with us.

"HOLY FUCKING SHIT HAWK! YOU DID IT!" Quinton shouts, kissing my cheek.

"NO, WE DID IT!" I shout to all of them with a smile so big my face hurts. "WE FUCKING DID IT!"

The team huddle doesn't let up for some time as we continue to celebrate and share in this magical moment for our team. All our hard work. All the long hours away from loved ones. All the hectic and busy schedules and we finally have something huge to show for it.

Mother fucker, does it feel good to be a Chicago Red Tail tonight.

It's another couple of hours before we're finally out of the arena but there's no way we're not celebrating at our home spot on the biggest win of our season. Pringle's is packed inside and out as fans celebrate with us. I've been dying to be alone with Rory tonight but understandably, she's been celebrating with Dex and Tatum. I got to hug her after the game and whisper to her how excited I was to get to take her home. I was happy to see her just as eager.

As fans disperse a little to let the team celebrate in our usual spot, I grab Rory under the pretense of needing a partner to play darts with me. Her water in hand, she giggles as she scoots out of the booth where she was sitting.

"You've had four beers tonight. You really think you're going to be any good at darts?"

I smirk at her judgement. "How about we make a bet?"

"Okay, what's the bet?"

"Head for the first one to hit the single ring."

"The single ring and not the bullseye?"

I laugh. "I mean I'm good, but I don't know if I'm that good on four beers."

She considers my proposal. "Alright. Deal."

Rory hits the single ring. I do not.

"Oooh, I'm so sorry," she laughs. "Looks like I get the tongue tonight."

"Wait, how about another bet."

She shakes her head in disbelief. "Alright, what's the bet this time Mr. Generous?"

"How about two orgasms before the other of us can orgasm. So, you'll get to come twice before I'm allowed and vice versa."

"My, my, my, you really are feeling generous tonight, Hawk. Alright. I'll take that bet. Give it your best shot."

I throw my dart and it banks off the plastic edge and falls to the floor.

She tosses hers and it hits almost dead center.

"Fuck," I mumble. "Alright another bet."

Laughing, she says, "You know you're just going to lose, Malone."

"I swear I've got it this time."

"Alright then wise guy. What's the bet?"

"How about you decide this one?"

"Hmm." she smirks. "Okay, if you hit the target, I'll make one of your sexual fantasies come true."

"Fuuuuck."

"Ah, ah, ah," she says, wagging her finger. "But if you miss and I make it, you make one of mine come true."

"Done!" I toss my dart at the board and it hits the fucking outer rim. "Shit!"

Rory merely smiles and then throws her dart with precision, raising her arms in celebration when it hits the inner ring of the target.

"Huzzah! Sweet success!"

"Fuck! One more."

"No way," she chides. "We're not playing until you win. You've already won huge tonight big guy."

I fold my hands together in front of her, pleading. "Please. Just one more. One more and that's it."

She sighs, but she's still smiling so I know she's having fun. "Alright, this is the final bet."

"Alright."

"What is it?"

"You have to hit the bullseye for this one."

Her brows shoot up. "Oooh, raising the stakes, eh?" She winks. "Let's hear it."

I lean in a little closer to her and say into her ear, "If I win, I will hunt you down and fuck you in this pub and you'll have to be quiet about it if you don't want anyone finding out."

"Well, that sounds like a win-win for me, Mr. Malone. Risky sex in public just happens to be my fantasy."

"Then throw your dart Lady Bug."

She focuses on her shot and then throws her dart but it bounces off the board and falls to the ground.

"Dammit."

Perfect.

She turns toward me with a shrug. "So, what happens if we both lose."

"Won't happen."

She cocks her head. "Come on. Be real. You're not very good at this."

I aim my dart and toss it forward, smirking when it hits the bullseye.

"What the..." Rory's jaw drops. "You played me!"

Her eyes flash with disbelief and amusement, but my stare back is nothing but hunger. With a slight raise of my brows, I whisper, "You might want to run."

She giggles. "Oh, my God, you're serious? Right now?"

"Right. Fucking. Now."

"Shit!" She turns and quickly bolts out of sight among the crowd, but I see where she's going and easily follow her toward the back of the pub, the both of us getting lost in the sea of people.

She traps herself in the back hallway, one door leading to the rest rooms, the other two leading to a supply closet and the walk-in cooler where the kegs are stored. The scene is set perfectly as she stands at one end of the hall and I at the other. One woman walks out of the bathroom as I begin to approach Rory, but with her phone in hand she doesn't pay us any attention. Rory turns her head left and right, unable to choose which path to take, so I swiftly take action, grabbing her hand and pulling her into the supply room before we're seen by anyone else.

Once inside, I lead her to the back of the space behind a set of shelves. She tries to speak but I instantly cover her mouth with my hand and lean her head back on my shoulder.

"Not a word, Lady Bug. Not one word."

I slip my other hand up the jersey she's wearing, the one with my name on it, and palm her breast. She melts against me with a soft moan.

"I've needed to put my hands on you all night. I can't fucking wait any longer."

I lower my hand from inside her shirt and slip it inside her leggings, beneath her thong, and between her legs. Her breathing picks up as I brush my fingers against her warm, wet flesh.

"Does this turn you on, Rory? The idea that we could get caught at any moment?"

She nods against my shoulder and gasps when I thrust my finger inside her.

"Christ, your pussy is so soft. So wet. I'm an addict, Rory. Addicted to your scent, your taste...the sound you make when you come. I. Can't. Get. Enough. Of. You."

She whimpers against me, my hand still against her mouth.

"Can I trust you not to make a sound? Because I really want to fuck you right here, but getting caught would be bad for both of us. Can I trust you, Rory?"

She reaches back behind her and brushes her hand over the stiff bulge in my pants and then she nods. I let go of her mouth and then kiss the back of her neck. "I want to fuck you just like this, Lady Bug. So, I can see my name across your back because you're mine, Rory. Say it."

Her thumbs inside the waistband of her leggings, she kicks off her heels and pulls them off, bending over and holding onto the shelf in front of her. She's naked from the waist down, now wearing nothing but my name in bold letters across her back.

"I'm yours Malone," she whispers. "What are you waiting for?"

Mother fuck.

She's so damn sexy.

I can't unzip my pants fast enough, freeing myself and palming my hardened shaft in my hand. A drop of silk dripping from the head of my cock, I slide it through her arousal, coating myself, and then sink inside her, as far as she'll take me.

"Good God," I whisper. "This feeling never gets old."

She gasps at first and then moans softly as she exhales. "Yes, Hawk...Please, more."

I continue with a slow and steady motion, pulsing in and out, in and out, allowing us both the moment to feel the absolute pleasure our bodies create together.

"Jesus, Rory. Do you feel this? You make me so goddamn hard. I will never not want you." It's a promise in the back of a supply closet during a risky quick fuck, I know, but it's a sincere promise all the same. I will never not want this girl. And I need her to know it.

"Hawken. Please don't stop." She breathes. "Please. I need more."

Me too, Babe. Me too.

Her words make me brave. Her plea makes me ravenous. I pick up my pace, thrusting into her, my hands gripping her hips and pulling her back against me with every move.

"Christ, Rory," I snarl as I buck my hips fast and furious. My lips separate and my head falls back as I soak in the sensation of my cock inside her. "You're so fucking perfect."

She's speechless, but I hear her breathing fast and deep right along with me as we chase our impending end. A lethal blend of white-hot heat and searing pleasure boils deep within my body and I'm ready for it.

Rory squeals out a whisper, "Hawk! I'm coming. Oh God, I'm coming!" Her body explodes, her magical pussy clamping down on my cock, squeezing it, pulling my orgasm from me.

And then the closet door opens.

My body is literally shaking as the supply closet door swings open. Hawken slams his hand over my mouth to stifle my pleasured groan and buries his head against my back as he wordlessly combusts, his cock pulsing inside me.

I'm sure my personality just split into two.

One is too ridiculously blissed out at the orgasm he just gave me to give two shits who stepped into this supply closet. The other is scared to death the lights will be flipped on and we'll be discovered as I stand here half naked.

That's what Dex and Hawken need right now. I can practically read the headlines already.

CHAMPIONSHIP HOCKEY STAR CAUGHT EXPOSING HIMSELF TO TEAMMATE'S SISTER.

Thank fucking Christ for darkened rooms.

Whoever entered the room is whistling to themselves as

they search the shelves for whatever they're looking for. Hawken and I are tucked away behind the very back set of shelves and I'm praying to everything that is spiritual or holy that whoever it is, they're not looking for condiments, silverware, or extra martini glasses.

I feel Hawken stiffen against me as we wait out our intruder.

No sudden movements.

No squeaks.

Don't even breathe.

"There you are." We hear the shifting of a cardboard box along with the rustling of plastic bags before the door finally clicks closed. Hawken sighs against me when the coast is clear and then he chuckles.

I turn swiftly and slap him on his upper arm. "Oh, my God! We almost got caught."

He shrugs, like he does this every day, and tucks himself back into his pants.

"But we didn't."

"But we could have!"

He lifts my chin with his finger and then kisses me like one satisfied and happy man.

"But we didn't."

He holds my leggings up for me and I step into them, pulling them up and putting myself back to normal.

"You are and will always be an amazing woman, Rory Foster. That was fun."

Even I must admit the thought of being caught, the idea that we just had this moment together with my brother less than fifty yards away and no clue, felt exhilarating. And for just a moment, right here in a public place, I was Hawken's and he was mine, because once we step out of this room, we're nothing but friends who occasionally hang out and fuck like rabbits.

When we exit the closet, I slip into the women's rest room so it doesn't look like we both came from the same place and who is in there?

Carissa, Tatum, and Charlee.

"Where have you been?" Tatum asks, fixing her hair in the mirror.

"Who me?"

"Yes." She laughs. "We were looking for you."

"I was playing darts with Hawken."

It's not a lie.

His penis was a nice dart and it hit the target perfectly.

"Fun! Who won?"

"Well, I did several times," I explain. "He kept pretending he sucked at the game, but then in the last round he hit the bullseye like he was slapping a puck into the net from a foot away. Totally played me."

Charlee smiles. "Ah, karma for what you did to him at the school festival perhaps?"

"Ha! Yeah, you're not wrong. I guess I deserved it."

"We were just talking about Key West and how we can't waaaaait to get on that plane."

"Right? Oh, my gosh. Sun, sand, all the day drinking we want. I'm ready for some R and R."

"Want to get together tomorrow to shop?" Carissa asks.

"Sure, I'm game! I need a couple new suits." Something that will make Hawken squirm.

"Great. I'll text you all in the morning and we'll make a plan."

"Don't call too early," Tatum orders. "I'm positive what Dex doesn't do to me tonight, he'll absolutely want to do in the morning."

I cover my ears with my hands. "Blah, blah, blah! I don't want to hear about my brother!"

Tatum laughs and swings the bathroom door open. Charlee follows her out and as I'm about to follow them, Carissa grabs my arm. When I turn around to face her, she's grinning at me like she knows a secret.

"What?"

"Oh, I just wanted to say next time you scratch the itch, you might want to make sure your leggings aren't inside out."

My jaw drops and my face turns beet red as I look down at my leggings.

Yep.

They are indeed inside out.

Shiiiiiit.

Cover blown.

She pretends to zip her lips and throw away the key and then she winks. "Hope it was fun."

"Reservation for Ben Dover." Dex winks at the guy behind the check-in counter who knows darn well who he is.

"Dude, seriously?" Milo lifts his brow. "Ben Dover?"

"What? It's how Tate and I met."

Hawken pounds the counter next to us. "Uuh, yeah,

my reservation is under Long Dong Silver. You got that in your little computer there?"

Long Dong Silver?

It takes all my self-control not to overreact to his made-up name. Instead, we all snicker like middle school kids but the hotel agent takes it all in stride. This is not his first rodeo with the Chicago Red Tails. Though it is the first time the team has a Championship cup to add to their list of accomplishments. The guys are on a high even a week after their winning game. This is the team's favorite Key West resort. They've been coming here for years at the end of each season and after finally winning the Cup this year, getting away from Chicago for a while is a well-deserved necessity.

The hotel agent smiles. "Ah, yes. Mr. Dover, Mrs. Dover, we've been expecting you. Here are your key cards and complimentary drink tokens. Your suite is all ready for you. Enjoy your stay. Mr. Silver, I think your name is in here somewhere. Let me just scroll...ah, yes. Here it is."

Milo's jaw falls open as he watches Dex and Hawken high five each other and then step back from the counter with their key cards. I roll my eyes and Charlee pats Milo's ass with a sweet smile after swallowing the few goldfish crackers she had tossed into her mouth.

"Don't worry, Babe. I've got you covered."

"What do you—"

"Fuck Norris please," she says to the hotel agent.

Milo bursts into a loud guffaw. "You seriously put our reservation under Fuck Norris?"

Charlee beams. "Do you seriously want the whole

world to know that *the* Milo Landric is staying in this very resort for the week?"

"No."

"Then yes."

Colby turns to Carissa. "So, what does that mean for us, Smalls? Did you give them a different name or am I boring old Colby?"

Carissa smirks and then gives her husband a kiss on the cheek. "Well, since I couldn't go with Thrill Drill..." The guys all snicker together. "I came up with my own name, just for you, babe."

She turns to the hotel agent and says, "Our reservation is under Duncan McKokinner, please."

"Oh, my God!" I howl in laughter with the girls.

The hotel agent nods. "Coming right up."

Carissa giggles and then glances at Colby. "It better be coming riiiiight up whenever I want."

"What about you, Miss?" The hotel agent smiles at me as I'm clearly not paired up with anyone in the group.

"Oh, you don't have to worry about me. Nobody knows me enough to care. It's just under Foster. Rory Foster."

"Very good, then. I've got your room key right here."

"Alright ladies," I exclaim, walking into Charlee and Milo's suite where we're hanging out for the afternoon. Their room has the best ocean view so we kicked the guys out for a few hours because girls' day. "I have all the necessary items for the best game of truth or dare ever!"

Carissa's eyes bulge at my three large grocery bags. "Truth or dare needs that many necessities?"

"Yep. Well, plus, I ordered the things you all requested as well and had them all delivered together. Sparkling water, chocolate bars, chocolate covered pretzels, popcorn, salt and vinegar chips, goldfish crackers..."

"Ooh! I'll take those!" Charlee reaches for the bag of crackers and a bottle of water while Carissa and Tatum grab some chocolate.

"Thanks Rory."

"Sure thing. So, who's going first?"

Tatum raises her hand. "I will."

"Truth or dare?"

"Ummm, how about truth?"

"Do my boobs look too big in this suit?" Charlee asks, standing and showing off her gorgeous new bikini.

Tate shakes her head. "Not at all. That blue looks amazing on you."

"Ugh, I feel like I'm bustin' out of it every time I look in the mirror."

Carissa laughs. "I hardly think Milo would have a problem with that."

Charlee waves her hands dismissively. "Sorry, that was probably way too easy of a truth but I needed an honest opinion." She sits back down as I stand.

"Well, if we're going in order, I guess that means I'm next."

"Okay then, truth or dare, Ror?" Tate pop a chocolate covered pretzel in my mouth.

"Let's go with dare. I don't really carry that many secrets."

"You don't, huh?" Tate winks at me but I confidently shake my head.

"Nope."

But if she only knew...

"Alright, let me think."

"No need. I've got one," Charlee announces. "Send a sexy text to one of the guys." She shares a mischievous glance with me and it's right this very second that I remember I once told her I had a small crush on Hawken.

Fucking Hell.

I can't even keep my own secrets.

"You have got to be kidding!" My eyes bulge and I shake my head.

"Yaaaaas!" Carissa nods with a maniacal laugh. "Oh, my God, that would be amazing! Oh, but don't send it to Colby obviously. He'll be pissed."

Tate cringes. "Well, she can't send one to her own brother."

"Milo will know she's joking," Charlee adds. "Oh, and don't send it to Zeke. He's not even here, so he could take it seriously." She narrows her eyes. "I mean unless that's something, you know, you feel like exploring?"

"Me and Zeke?" I scowl, but not because I don't like Zeke. On the contrary, I think he's a fantastic guy and despite all the bullshit he's been handed, he's a wonderful father to his little girl. I've simply never thought of him in any other way as a friend of my brother's and player on the team.

"No! Of course not. I mean, I love Zeke. He's a great guy and an amazing player, but no." I shake my head. "I'm not his type."

"Well, that leaves Hawken or Quinton, and Quinton isn't coming till tomorrow sooo, I guess that only leaves you one choice." Carissa smirks at me like she knows she's got me in check mate.

It's not like Hawken won't enjoy a sexy text from me. Maybe I can play with him a little and see what happens. The girls don't have to know exactly what's going on between us and even Carissa doesn't know every single thing. As long as I never pick truth, I won't have to divulge that information.

I roll my eyes and grab my phone off the table. "Alright. What do I say in this text?"

Charlee pops up and steps onto the balcony looking down at where the guys are seated by the pools overlooking the beach.

"Oooh I got it! Write this. 'Just tell me to S-T-F-U-A-T-T-D-L-A-G-G'."

"What does that spell?"

She smirks. "It doesn't spell anything. If you know, you know."

"Well, clearly I don't know! What the fuck, Charlee?" I laugh nervously, my cheeks heating. "What am I saying to him? Will he know what it means?"

She shrugs. "Just do it and don't worry about it. One day you'll thank me."

"What the fuck," I mumble as I type out the text and press send. We all quietly race to the balcony to see Hawken pull his phone from his pocket and read his text. He looks around and then slides his phone back into his pocket without a reply, but I'll be damned if we don't all witness him adjusting himself in his swim trunks and that's enough to put us all into a fit of giggles.

"Alright Carissa," I say, turning to her. "You're next. Truth or dare?"

"Truth, please."

I think for a moment and then ask, "Where's the last place you and Colby did the deed while on this vacation?"

A wicked smile plays across Carissa's face. "In the ocean this morning when we went for a dip to watch the sunrise."

We all applaud. "Very nice! I like it!"

"Charlee's turn," I declare. "Truth or dare?"

"Truth!"

Tatum doesn't hesitate. "Are you pregnant?"

All eyes shoot to Tate and Charlee's smile falters. "What? No!"

"Are you sure about that?"

Her eyes the size of saucers, she asks Tate, "Why would you ask?"

She shrugs. "Just being observant. You said you feel like you're busting out of your bikini. You've been craving gold-fish crackers like crazy which is what I ate when I was pregnant with Summer, and you haven't had a drop of alcohol since we've been here."

"Wine has been making me feel very flushed lately. And tired."

Carissa gasps. "Oooh and you weren't feeling good the other day, remember? At dinner?"

"Ooof." Charlee frowns. "That fish smelled terrible. Can you blame me?"

"Have you tested?"

She turns back to Tate. "No. I..." She shakes her head and then finally sighs and leans back on the couch. "I'm too scared to take a test."

The vibe in the room changes for all of us as we come to our friend's aid. We all know Charlee went through hell and back when she was younger and that she most likely can't have kids. It's gut-wrenching.

"Noo, Charlee, why are you afraid?" I smooth my hand down Charlee's arm.

"Because our first round of IVF failed and it was devastating."

"But sweetheart, that doesn't mean it will fail every time? Did you guys do another round?"

"No. I wanted to take a few months off before we start up again because I hate feeling like a failure."

"You're not a failure, Charlee. Let's get that out of your head right now. And what about your period?" Tate asks her.

"A week ago."

"Oh."

"No. I mean, I was due a week ago. And it never came."

We collectively gasp. "Charlee! Are your cycles usually off?"

She shakes her head. "In the past year they've been like clockwork."

"Then this could be it! You have to take a test."

"No way. Not here." She folds her arms across her chest. "I don't want to ruin our vacation if it's not the answer we want."

"Does Milo know your period is late?"

"No. I mean he's smart enough to figure it out if he

wants to, but I don't always talk about it and I really didn't want him to get his hopes up. He really wants to be a dad and I want more than anything to be able to make it happen for him."

Tate leans over and grabs her hand. "If I go downstairs to the little pharmacy and pick up a test, will you take it? Just for us? You don't have to tell Milo a thing if you don't want to."

"I don't know."

"How about if everyone takes one?" I suggest.

Charlee frowns. "What?"

"Well, maybe not me, because I was literally just on my period so I'm for sure not pregnant but if it'll make it easier for you if Carissa and Tate take one, I'll go get them." I nudge Charlee. "Come on, it'll be fun. Just us. No guys!"

It takes a little more convincing but Charlee finally relents and I happily run downstairs to the pharmacy to purchase a few tests. While I'm checking out, my phone dings, alerting me to a text.

HAWKEN

D-Y-W-M-T-C-O-A-E-Y-P-T-Y-C-O-M-F?
😏 L-Y-H-F-M-L.

What the hell could all those letters mean?

What is he trying to tell me and why do I have a sneaky suspicion it's downright dirty?

Before I head back up to the room, I first Google what my message to him meant, snorting when I see the result.

S-T-F-U-A-T-T-D-L-A-G-G: Shut the fuck up and take this dick like a good girl.

Bringing my palm to my forehead, I shake my head at my own ignorance.

"I should've figured that one out. Nicely done, Charlee."

Too eager to see what Hawken's message is, I research it too.

Do you want me to come over and eat your pussy till you come on my face? Lift your hips for me, Love.

"Hooooly shit." I fan myself. "How did he know to respond that way?"

"He either Googled it himself or..." I think about it a moment and realize who he was sitting next to at the pool.

That has to be it. "Milo."

"Fuck me," I mumble, giggling to myself over Hawken's response. The lady behind the counter who takes my payment for the pregnancy tests, raises a brow.

"You know saying things like that is what leads to buying tests like these."

Realizing she heard me talking to myself, I snicker and explain the tests actually aren't for me. Who cares if she believes me or not?

One by one my three friends use the restroom and pee on their respective sticks. Tate takes it in stride as does Carissa because neither of them have been trying to get pregnant. I imagine though, Charlee's nerves are through the roof right now.

"Okay so all tests go face down on this placemat." I point to the green woven placemat on the table. "We'll wait three minutes and then turn them over."

When the timer dings on my phone, they turn their tests over, all peering at Charlee's results.

Two pink lines.

Two noticeably clear pink lines.

Tears roll down her face and then she collapses into sobs as we all rally around her, hugging her, comforting her, crying with her, and celebrating with her.

"How is this even possible?" she wails. "This shouldn't be happening."

"But it is, Charlee! It is!" Tate squeals. "You deserve this happiness, babe. Take it! Miracles can happen every day!"

"Yeah." Carissa nods. "Maybe all the medicine you were taking helped reset your body or something."

I shrug with a smirk. "Or maybe Jared was always the infertile one and you just never knew it." They all look at me knowing I could very well be right.

"Wouldn't that just be the karma that man deserves." Charlee chuckles through her sniffles. "Shootin' blanks all his life."

Tate picks up Charlee's test and hands it to her. "Well Milo certainly does not shoot blanks and you have your proof right here!"

I peer down at the rest of the tests expecting to see only one line on each of them, but that is not the case.

Holy shit.

Is this seriously happening?

"Ummm, he's not the only one who carries strong swimmers." I pick up the remaining tests from the table and turn them around.

"Positive...and...positive."

Tate's smile falters as shock sets in. "Wait, what?"

"You have got to be kidding." Carissa's jaw hangs open as I wave their tests in the air.

The cackle that comes from my mouth as I stand here staring back at three shocked pregnant women is unbelievable.

"Read 'em and weep, bitches! Y'all are knocked all the way up! All of you!" I clap my hands and jump up and down like a giddy schoolgirl. "It's going to be the year of the crazy baby train! Oh, my GOD! I'm going to be an aunt three times in one year! What even is this life?"

"You ladies better be ready for dinner because we are starving!" Colby barges into the room with the rest of the guys in tow. Dex wraps a possessive arm around Tate's waist and kisses her temple.

"Hell, yeah, and it's all you can eat surf and turf night!" I hear Hawken say.

"Ready in a minute, gentlemen," Carissa tells them as she steps out of the bathroom with me after applying her makeup.

Colby's eyes light up when he sees his wife. "Hubba, hubba, Smalls. You look hot."

"Thank you, Babe. You don't look so bad, yourself."

Hawken's hungry eyes drag up and down my body, checking out my black strapless maxi dress with tropical flowers flowing across the bottom hem. I can only imagine what he might be thinking given our text exchange earlier.

Eat your heart out Mr. Malone.

"I just need to grab my shoes from the balcony," Tate tells Dex as Charlee emerges from the bedroom in her newest yellow sundress to Milo's appreciation.

There's a flurry of activity around the room as we all grab shoes or purses or last-minute accessories before heading down to dinner together. Dex follows Tate toward the balcony but stops short.

"Holy shit! What the hell is this? Who's pregnant?"

A collective "What?" comes from the other guys as Dex picks up the three pregnancy tests that were left on the table. He looks at me and shit, Hawken is looking like he might pass out.

I lift my hands. "Don't look at me. I'm not pregnant."

I notice Hawken closes his eyes and breathes a sigh of relief.

Carissa shrugs playfully and then steps forward. "Oh, sorry. This one is mine," she says, pulling one of the tests from Dex's hand.

"What the fuck?" Colby gasps with a huge goofy smile on his face. "Are you serious?"

Tate doesn't wait for Carissa's reaction before she follows suit and steps up behind Dex, pulling another stick from his grasp. "And this one is mine."

Dex's mouth opens and his jaw drops as he turns to her, not paying attention to the fact the third test was just pulled from his hand.

"Babe!"

Tate beams back at him with a playful lift of her shoulder. "There must be something in the water here."

"Holy shit!" He pulls her into a hug and I beam at both

of my friends, sharing in their excitement. I turn to step over next to Hawken and it's then that I see it.

Our friends, Charlee and Milo.

Tate sees them too and turns Dex around so he can watch.

Milo stares at the test now in his hands, his brows pinched. His eyes wide. "Is this for real?"

Charlee sniffles and nods. "You couldn't pay me enough to joke about this, Milo."

Tears fall from his eyes and he doesn't try to stop them. "But we didn't..."

"I know," Charlee answers his unfinished sentence.

"But I thought—"

"Me too."

He glances down at the test again and then stares at Charlee. "Babe...we're going to be parents?"

"We're going to be parents. We did it, Milo."

"You're really pregnant?"

She laughs this time. "I'm really pregnant."

Milo pulls her into his arms, kissing her and smoothing his thumbs over her cheeks to dry her tears.

"And Carissa is really pregnant," Charlee announces. "And Tate is really pregnant...again."

I flail my arms, pointing at each of them like I'm Oprah Winfrey herself. "YOU get a baby! And YOU get a baby! EVERYBODY GETS A BABAAAAAY!"

Everyone laughs and Hawken shakes his head. "You all are just over here creating the next generation of Red Tails one kid at a time, eh?"

17

HAWKEN

What the fuck is going on inside my brain that has me questioning everything about my relationship with Rory?

I just stood in a room upstairs and watched three of my friends find out they're about to be fathers, having never once considered the possibility of Rory getting pregnant during any of our times together. The agreement Rory and I discussed a while back was one made from pure lust. We didn't discuss the possible physical consequences of our actions. I never considered Rory's health.

The only person we really considered was Dex.

How could I have been so selfish?

Rory said she's not pregnant and that she didn't take a test, but is she sure about that?

Maybe she should have taken one anyway.

Why didn't she?

And if she had and the test would've been positive... fuck, what would she think then?

Hearing her say she wasn't pregnant was a relief to my

system at first. Good God, I would never want to hurt her or put her in a predicament she's not ready for, but also, watching my friends accept their new realities with excitement and hope is making me a feel a whole other way I hadn't thought about before. Now here I am, seated with them in the resort restaurant wondering how I might have reacted had Rory told me she was carrying my child.

And fuck, I think I would've been okay with it.

Happy even.

And actually, it may have even helped bridge the issue of Rory wanting to hide everything from Dex. Sure, he would probably be pissed at first, but it wouldn't take him long to get over it. Not when his sister is pregnant and emotional. He loves her too much to stay mad at her...and therefore, hopefully me as well.

That's probably a shitty thing to say.

Hell, how did I get here?

How did I go from wanting Rory any time I could get her to being somewhat disappointed there's no baby for us to celebrate?

How did I go from feeling relief hearing she's not pregnant to wishing even a tiny bit that she was?

I would make an excellent father, but more than anything, as I sit here now watching her talk with her friends and her brother, and from watching my teammates with their wives and partners, I'm convinced, I want what they have.

Someone they can love who loves them just as equally.

Stable, committed relationships.

And now, growing families.

And I really want those things with Rory.

"To happy accidents and our new tiny miracles." Colby leads everyone at the table in a toast. "And to winning the Cup and getting a well-deserved recharge in this beautiful town."

"Here, here!" Everyone raises their glasses and passes their cheers across the table. I clink glasses with Rory seated catty-cornered to me. As if my life is happening in slow motion, she glances at me, her long eyelashes bouncing off her sun-kissed cheeks. A knowing smile passes between us but hell if I know what she might be thinking.

Is she wondering what I would've thought about a baby the way I'm thinking about it?

Is she thinking about the texts we exchanged earlier today that we still haven't talked about?

Whatever it is, I wish I could read her thoughts.

I take a sip of my wine before lowering my glass to the table and then pick up my phone and send her a text.

ME

You look beautiful tonight.

RORY

You don't look so bad yourself.

ME

You going to need help getting that off tonight? I might be available.

RORY

I suppose I might need help getting off.

ME

😋 I think you forgot a word in that last text, Lady Bug.

RORY

😊 I think I didn't.

"You know you two are making faces right here at the table, right?" Milo whispers in my ear.

"Huh?"

"Yeah." He nods. "You two are the only ones with your phones out and you both have shit-eating grins. It's not hard to figure out you're talking to each other."

"Fuck. Sorry."

He nudges me with his elbow. "Just pointing out the obvious before your buddy Dex does."

"Thanks."

Pocketing my phone, I wipe my mouth with my napkin and give one more glance to Rory before turning my attention away from her and back to the rest of our friends.

My hotel room door clicks open and then closed. I know it's Rory because I slipped her my key earlier this evening. She finds me lounging on the balcony overlooking the ocean which can no longer be seen against the night sky, but the sound of the waves is eerily calming.

"Hey Sexy. What are you doing out here?" Her question is sincere, her tone slightly worrisome. "Are you alright?"

"Yeah, I'm fine. Why do you ask?"

She lays a hand on my bare shoulder and hitches a leg over me, lifting her dress as she straddles my lap on the lounge chair. Instinctively, I bring my hands around her ass, holding her against me. I like that she's comfortable being with me like this.

"You weren't downstairs at the bar," she explains. "I thought maybe you fell asleep or didn't feel well or something."

I inhale a deep breath, breathing Rory in as I hold her. The scent of coconut wafting through my nose. "Nah. Just relaxing up here. Thinking."

"Thinking about what?"

"You. Us."

She leans back a smidge. "Me? What about me?"

"Earlier, before supper," I mention, referring to the girls and all their pregnancy chaos.

"Yeah." She grins and huffs out a laugh. "I saw the relief on your face when I said I wasn't pregnant. Sorry to not give you any warning. You probably almost had a heart attack."

Still not totally sure how to express my feelings to her, I nod slowly. "I guess my first instinct was to be relieved yeah, but then I started thinking about it. Thought about it all through dinner."

Her brow peaks. "About what? Me being pregnant?"

"Yeah."

"You want me to be pregnant?" she asks with complete shock on her face. "Have you..." She cocks her head. "Have you been trying to knock—"

"No, no, no, no, no. God. Fuck...no. I'm sorry. I'm not doing the best job explaining myself here, Ror, but no. I've never been anything but honest with you."

Fuck. That's a lie.

"And I would never want to put you into a predicament you don't want to be in."

"Okay..."

"But I'm curious what your reaction would have been had you taken a test and found out it was positive."

She cups my face in her hands. "Hawk, I didn't need to take a test because my period just ended. The last time we had sex was at Pringle's, remember? And then my period came. I mean, I know weird things can happen but there's pretty much no chance I'm pregnant right now."

"Okay, but for shits and giggles, if you were..."

"Would I be okay with it?"

I nod, swallowing a lump in my throat. "Yeah."

Without answering, she studies my face and then asks, "Would you?"

"Truth?"

"Always."

I smooth her dark waves from her face, my eyes darting between hers. "The truth is, there is no one better to be the mother of my children than you, Rory Foster."

Her eyes bulge and her lips separate. "Wha-what?"

I give her a helpless smile. "You're a beautiful soul, Rory. Kind, compassionate, nurturing, friendly..."

"But Hawk—"

"I'm in love with you, Rory."

As if I took the wind out of her sails, she sits back, speechless, shaking her head in disbelief.

"Maybe I shouldn't be telling you any of this, and I'm sorry if my doing so is hurting you in any way but fuck it. I need to get this off my chest because it's been weighing me down for far too long."

"Hawk..."

"I love you, Rory." I chuckle lightly, again, because I'm a nervous, helpless bastard. "I think I've been in love with you for years. You've become a part of me...a part of my family and I think...I think somehow, I always knew in my heart I would get to share life with you and for the longest time I convinced myself it would only ever be as Dex's little sister. But then..." My breathing is becoming erratic the more I try to say what's on my mind. It's all coming out like one big word-vomit.

"But then this past year, we grew closer, and...and then I found The Hawk in your bedroom and I knew, Rory. I knew then, you had to feel the same way somewhere right here." I flatten my hand over her heart.

"And then we danced and..." I shake my head, my eyes squeezing closed. "And it was fucking amazing and then I kissed you because I just couldn't keep my feelings to myself any longer."

I watch as a tear slips down Rory's cheek, catching it with the pad of my thumb. "And then that night at the game. Fuck, Rory, my heart burst into pieces when I saw you were hurt. I wanted to get to you in any way I could, hockey be damned, because you're more important to me than anything I could ever do on that ice, but I was trapped. There was nothing I could do but get myself to that sin bin so I could see you. I never wanted a game to end as fast as I did that night."

She sniffles and I catch a few more tears. "Hawk..."

I shake my head. "Let me finish. I need to say all this, Ror."

She gives me a tiny nod.

"Lying next to you in my bed that night, taking care of you...it was the single best thing to ever happen to me. And it didn't need to be any more than that. I knew you were safe in my arms and that's all that mattered, but then..."

"The shower," she whispers.

"The shower. I snapped, Ror. I couldn't hold back anymore. You were too perfect and I needed to show you how much you meant to me...but then..." I shake my head, trying to keep my voice steady. "Fuck."

"Hawken," Rory cries. "I am so sorry."

"I know you want this to be a friends-with-benefits kind of thing, but I just can't do it anymore, Rory. I hate this arrangement. I hated it at the very beginning and I hate it now. I only agreed to it because it meant I got to have you to myself for however long you would give me, but fuck it all now, because I can't do it anymore. I love you. I'm in love with you and I want you. All of you. I want a life with you. A forever with you. And I want the world to know it. I want your brother to know it. You're one of my best friends and you're unequivocally the only lover I will ever want again and if Dex can't handle that then too fucking bad."

She stares at me, tears rolling down her beautiful face.

I try to wipe some of them away but many more trickle down in their place. "Don't cry, Lady Bug. I didn't mean to make you cry. Just...be with me, Rory. Be my person, my partner, my lover. Be mine. And allow me to be yours."

Her beautiful brown eyes stare back at me as she cries what I'm sure are happy tears. "I love you too, Hawk. I've always loved you."

"Rory." Her name is a sigh on my lips as I brush them against hers. "I love you so fucking much."

"Touch me, Hawken," she whispers against my mouth. "I need this moment with you."

With her straddled across my lap, I gently dust her neck and shoulders in slow, deliberate kisses. Tasting her skin with every brush of my lips. She tilts her head to the side and back allowing my access. Slipping two fingers into the bust line of her dress, I pull the top down exposing an entirely new surprise.

"Did you wear this for me?" I ask as I expose the entirety of the black one-piece lingerie set she's wearing.

Something more than seduction flashes in her eyes this time. The raw emotion alone tugs at my chest. "Only for you."

"Christ, Rory."

How is a man supposed to have any control like this?

She's got me wrapped around her proverbial finger. God, I've longed for this moment so fucking much. She has to feel this is more than just sex for me. I want her body, yes, but more than that, I want her soul. I want her heart. I want every fucking piece of Rory Foster I can get.

My arms wrapping around her, I lift her from my lounge chair and carry her inside, kicking the door closed behind me. "Nobody gets to see this but me."

"Always you, Hawken."

I sit on the edge of the bed keeping her on my lap, my lips crashing against hers and I do not let go. We spend several long minutes tasting each other, our lips separating, our tongues dancing a slow seductive dance before I finally twist our bodies and lay her out on my bed.

"Let me look at you, Lady Bug."

Sprawled out below me, her smile is a haze of emotion

and hunger. "Fucking gorgeous." Hovering over her, I kiss her forehead and then work my way down to her nose, her warm cheeks, the curve of her neck, and then I lick along the top of her lingerie, teasing her skin with what's to come.

"Hawk..." My name is her breath and fuck, it's the most heavenly sound I could ever hear.

Feathering my fingers over her lingerie, I circle my fingers around her nipples and nip them with my teeth over the lacey material. Lying beside her, she explores my upper body while I unclasp her lingerie one at a time down her abdomen. When it finally falls open I wrap my hand around one of her bared breasts, holding it in my palm, squeezing and dusting my thumb over her nipple. Her sharp gasp is the response I was looking for.

She takes a purposely slow breath and caresses the back of my head as I hover over her and nuzzle my face between her breasts, kissing each one and christening her tight peaks with my tongue. Her nails feel incredible as she drags them through my hair, but it's the helpless whimper and accompanying moan coming from her that tells me all I need to know.

"I love you, Hawk. I've always loved you."

"More?"

"Yes," she whispers. "Please."

I bring my mouth over her nipple, lapping at the nub over and over again, grazing it with my teeth and then sucking hard, her back arching off the bed in response.

"Jesus, Hawk."

"You're so goddamn beautiful, Rory."

I move to her other breast and repeat my movements.

Lick.

Nip.

Suck.

Gasp.

Moan.

I work my way back up her body, kissing her lips again and then dragging my tongue to her ear, nibbling on her earlobe. "Are you wet for me, Rory?"

Her legs fall open in anticipation. "You know I am."

I bring her hand to my shorts, helping to push her hand down inside. "See what you do to me, Ror?" I breathe against her as her hand wraps around my stiff cock. "You get me so fucking hard. Uncomfortably so. It's torturous in the best way."

As she drags her fingers down and around my balls, cupping me in her hands and squeezing my shaft, I feather my fingers along her pussy, her arousal coating me in seconds. I dip my head to the crook of her neck, trying like hell to rein in my control when I feel her.

"Goddamn, Rory," I pant. "You're so...fuck...I need to taste you."

Trying not to scramble, I kiss and nip my way down her body, past her hip until I reach my target. Her body writhes underneath me.

"Hawken..."

"Do you want my tongue, Rory?"

"You know I do. Please, Hawk."

I take one look at her gorgeous glistening pussy and shake my head. "As much as I like to play with my food before I eat it, I don't think I can manage it this time, Ror."

"Hawken!" she cries.

Fuck it.

I need her.

Need to taste her.

Satisfy her.

Love her.

With no other warning, I spread her legs and trail my tongue through her sweet pussy in one long flattened stroke.

"Oh...my...God!" She moans, her body writhing against my face.

Sweet Jesus, she is everything.

I reach the apex and swirl my tongue around and over her clit, and then drag my tongue down and back up all over again.

And then I suck.

And lick.

And suck.

And lick.

And suck.

"Hawken! Oh, God! Yes!"

Fuck, my cock is so hard. If I don't find some relief soon, I might combust, but with every gasp, every moan, every whimper that comes from her mouth, I lose a bit more of my control and know the moment I push myself inside her, I'll be a dead man walking.

"Fuuuuck, Hawk. I'm...I'm...Oh God, I'm right there." Her chest heaves with every breath and she's completely lost the ability to keep her body still as she writhes against my face.

"Then let go, babe. Let me feel you come on my tongue."

Though I know I don't need to, I push two fingers

inside her, curving them up against her inner wall with just enough pressure while I devour her clit until she screams and her body tenses around my fingers. She pushes her hand through my hair, grasping onto the strands as she comes apart on my face, my tongue continuing to lap up every drop until she can stand it no longer.

As she recovers from her high, I stand from the bed momentarily and push my briefs down, stepping out of them, and then grip my cock in my hand. Rory eyes my erection with a darkened, hungry glare.

"Don't look at me like that, Lady Bug. This will end up going much faster than either of us wants it to go."

She licks her lips, never once making eye contact with me.

Fuck me, she has eyes for one thing and one thing only.

"I want that cock, Hawken. In my mouth. Right fucking now."

18

RORY

Hawken crawls onto the bed in all his naked glory, kneeling next to me as I sit up. I reach out to grip his cock in my hands and he hisses in response, his head falling back.

"Fuck, Rory."

I smooth my hand up and down his velvety shaft, drag my tongue lazily from root to tip, and then lower my lips over his head.

"Goddamn..."

Hawken slides his hand into my hair, watching in awe as I take him in inch by inch until he hits the back of my throat. "Fucking beautiful, Ror. You take my cock like it was made just for you. Only you, babe."

Sliding back, I wrap my hand around the base of this shaft and take him into my mouth again, my tongue dragging across his sensitive skin, licking the beads of precum waiting as I reach the tip again. With his hands on the back my head, he doesn't push me but holds my hair back so he can get a perfect view as I suck him off. His moan of approval makes me wet all over again. Picking up my pace, I squeeze him between my lips, a few sloppy sucking sounds emanating from my mouth much to his pleasure.

"So, fucking sexy. Take it all, Lady Bug. Take my cock as I fuck your sweet mouth."

I moan while he's in my mouth, the vibrations of my voice spurring him on as he begins to thrust lightly, pushing himself inside me until he hits the back of my throat.

"Yesssss."

Finally, he pulls out of me and sits on the bed, pulling me across him so I'm straddling him once again. "I don't want to come in your mouth, babe. I want to be inside you when I explode. Put me inside you."

God yes.

I can't wait for him to fill me.

To feel him inside me while I move against him.

To squeeze his thick cock when I come all over him for a second time.

I sit up on my knees and position him at my entrance, his jaw clenching at the feeling of how wet I am again. And then I sink over him inch by delicious inch, both of us speechless as we bask in the pleasure of our bodies becoming one.

"So, fucking tight," he murmurs. "Are you okay?"

"Sooo much more than okay, Hawk."

He reaches up and takes my breasts in his hands. "This is how I want to fuck you, Rory. Goddamn, I want to watch you come undone knowing it was my cock that did it to you."

My head falls back when he pinches my nipples. "Oh, my God..."

"Incredible, Lady Bug. Fucking Incredible."

"I need to move, Hawk."

"You don't need my permission, babe. Take my cock as hard and fast as you want it."

God. Yes!

He meets my every movement with a flex of his hips, his eyes laser focused on watching his cock fill me with every thrust. I lean back just a bit, my hands grasping Hawken's thighs. His strong arms reach out to me, his hands palming my breasts as we move together and oh, my God, I think I might be having an out of body experience.

"It's so good...Hawk!" I breathe. "So, fucking good."

He grips my hips as I move faster over him, racing for the amount of friction I need to reach the climax we both desire.

"Ride me, Rory. Fucking ride me and don't you stop until you're screaming my name."

Our skin smacks together as I bounce my body up and down over him and then suddenly, he's sitting up, wrapping his arms around my body, holding me tightly against him. And then his mouth is on mine.

"God, Rory. I can't get enough of you. I love you so goddamn much."

"Hawken."

"Need you...want you. Can't breathe without you."

"Oh, my God...Yes. Fuck...yes...Hawken I'm going to... I'm...God, I'm..." He thrusts into me once, twice, three more times and then I'm clenching around his cock, his name tumbling from my lips. I wrap my arms tightly around his neck, not wanting to ever let go as his cock pulses and he comes apart inside me.

"Fuuuuuucking hell," he grinds out, his arms so tight around me I nearly lose my ability to breathe. He pulses a few more times and I rest my head in the crook of his neck, kissing him tenderly until he calms enough to lie back, keeping me on top of him and refusing to let go.

"That was...fuuuck," he pants, his heart pounding underneath me.

"Yeah." That's all I can say because no way in hell can I form a coherent sentence right now.

Hawken Malone just took my body, my heart, my soul, and apparently my words because I currently have zero thoughts running through my brain and don't think I could conjure a coherent one if I tried.

My eyes spring open at some point during the night far from dawn given the amount of darkness surrounding me. I've tossed and turned more than a few times over the past couple hours and I just can't do it anymore. Hawken is breathing peacefully beside me, completely oblivious to the anxiety swirling in my head.

Why does everything have to feel so complicated?

"I'm in love with you, Rory."

"I'm in love with you and I want you. All of you. I want a life with you. A forever with you. And I want the world to know it. I want your brother to know it."

It's always Dex, isn't it?

He's the sole reason I'm awake in the middle of the night lying next to the one man who has never treated me like Dex's little sister. He's never used me to get to my brother. Never made me feel less than because I'm not the wealthy star hockey player he is. He's a man who loves the sport but shows sincere interest in me and what I do. I should be head over heels and blissfully happy right now. Hawken loves me.

And I love him too.

I wish more than anything things could work with us, but I'm just not sure my heart can trust that in the end, he won't choose my brother over me. How can he not when they literally play on the same team? When they have to work closely together to bring home the win. It's their job. Their livelihood. Their passion.

I never tried to barge in on Dex and Hawken's friendship. Though he was always kind and friendly to me, I always tried to remain on the outside with my own friends. My own life. Dex has done enough for me over the years. The last thing he needs or deserves is a nagging little sister tagging along to everything he does. But when Hawken came to the Red Tails, we all sort of clicked. When he was around my brother, he treated me like another one of his friends even when I was simply curled up on the couch watching T.V. trying to not barge in.

Though we never meant for anything to happen in the beginning, I think there's been this magnetic pull between us for years. An attraction built on such a strong years-long friendship, it was inevitable we would end up together at some point.

But now that we're in the spot to make things real, I'm scared to death to take the leap.

I know he loves me, but what if he meets someone else?

SUSAN RENEE

What if something happens between us and it drives a wedge between us? Where does that leave Dex? Or what if something goes awry between my brother and me? Or even Dex and Hawken? A falling out in the years to come. How would they ever be able to work together?

It breaks my heart, even though nothing has happened yet, to think it would be my fault either of them would ever have to worry about these types of situations happening. And maybe Hawken hasn't considered any of this yet because he's blinded by love and lust. He's not thinking clearly.

A couple rebel tears slip down my cheeks.

I don't want to do this.

I don't want to leave this room.

I don't want to walk away from him.

But what other choice do I really have?

For Hawk's sake and for Dex's.

Slipping quietly out of bed, I reach for my things and walk out of Hawken's hotel room for the last time.

They say all magic comes with a price.

Whoever *they* were, I want to light them on fire and watch them burn because I'm now paying the price for the most magical couple of months I could've ever asked for.

Am I doing the right thing? Hell, if I know.

But as much as it hurts right now, I know I'm protecting my heart from the inevitable crash and burn that would come later. And protecting my heart as well as those of Hawken and Dex is always the right choice.

I hold myself together until the moment my hotel room door closes, at which point I slide down the backside of the door in a crumbled mess of tears and pain. I could grab a

238

ride to the airport early and see about flying home, but that will only make Dex worry. Since there's zero reason for my needing to return home before the team, I'm going to have to tough it out. In a few short hours, Hawken will wake up and not understand why I'm not there. He'll be devastated or pissed...or both, and I'll have to figure out how to navigate that, but for now, I just want to cry myself to sleep.

19

HAWKEN

Last night was without a doubt the best night of my life, championship cup be damned. I finally told Rory how I felt about her. Made love to her several times over and fell asleep with her wrapped in my arms. Everything was just as it should be. Rory and I, blissfully happy and ready to tell the world we're in love. I've wanted her for years, and until recently I never allowed myself to think about the real possibility of having a life with her. But when it's right, it's right.

I'm in love with Rory Foster.

So why am I sitting up in bed this morning completely alone with no trace of her in my room?

"What the fuck?" I murmur to myself, shoving my hand through my messy bed head.

Wait.

Don't overreact.

Maybe she woke early and went for a walk.

I check my phone for any missed texts but my screen is blank.

Okay...it could literally be nothing.

She could be changing or grabbing coffee.

> Morning gorgeous. I missed you leaving this morning. Assuming you went to change. Want to meet for breakfast?

She doesn't reply to my text which gives me an uneasy feeling.

Did she leave for a different reason?

No, no, no, no, no. We went over this last night.

We're good.

Everything is fine.

Right. So why am I throwing on my clothes, fixing my hair, and bolting out the door to go find my girl like last night never really happened?

I run down to the beach wondering if I might find her jogging or looking at shells but she's nowhere to be found. I pass by the pool area and don't see her resting in the hot tub, nor is she in the gym. The last place I look is the breakfast buffet and that's exactly where I find her. Seated in a booth with her brother...blowing her nose and wiping tears from her face.

What the hell?

My feet act of their own accord carrying me across the room. I'm just about to interrupt their conversation and ask Rory what's wrong when Dex spots me.

"Hey Hawk!" He waves me over. "Come join us."

My glance shoots to Rory sitting across from him, her red rimmed eyes and flush face staring back at me.

Why is she crying?

"Rory?" I cock my head, my brows pinched together. "What's going o—"

"She's having guy problems."

What?

Guy problems?

What the fuck is he talking about?

I open my mouth to ask what the fuck Dex is talking about when she meets my gaze again giving me a subtle headshake. I watch her take a deep breath and brush a few more tears from her cheeks.

Dex doesn't know?

She hasn't told him?

Or maybe she did tell him and this is how he's reacting?

I don't know what the hell is going on.

What happened between her falling asleep in my arms last night and her here with her brother crying over...me?

Dex takes another bite of his bagel and pats the seat next to him. "Come on. You and I can try to put my sister back together. We're good at this man shit."

Fuuuuuck. He doesn't know.

This is really happening right now.

Something in my stomach turns and I feel like I could throw up. My skin is clammy and I'm starting to sweat. Hell, if I move even an inch, I might not be able to control what happens next.

"Dude, you alright, man? You don't look so hot."

"Ah, yeah," I muster. "Hungry I think."

I'm not the least bit hungry.

How could I even think of eating right now when the girl I was making love to last night is now sitting here teary-eyed and not talking to me?

My God, did I hurt her?

Did I not give her enough?

Was everything she said a lie?

"Well, go fill yourself a plate. The eggs are surprisingly good and the hashbrowns are perfection."

I slip into the booth right next to Dex across from Rory where I can see her face. "I'll wait. What's uh...what's going on, Rory?"

She knows I hate this pretending game, yet here I am, forced to pretend I didn't almost come in her mouth last night. Forced to pretend I know nothing of her feelings. Forced to pretend I'm not falling apart on the inside as my heart splinters into tiny shards.

"Mmm." Dex wipes his mouth with his napkin. "Cliff Notes version. She's been talking to a guy and thought there was really something there but she's too scared to take the leap because if it doesn't work out it would hurt more than just the two of them, but she sees what Tatum and I have and Milo and Charlee and even Colby and Carissa and she wants that too." He lays his hand over hers on the table and inside my jealousy is screaming because I want to touch her too. "She deserves that kind of happiness. I promise you're going to find it, Ror."

She can have it now!

She can have it all with me!

I could give her the world!

I want to give her everything!

What the fuck is even happening right now?

Swallowing my emotions, I lean back against the booth and stare her down. "Tell me about this guy. What's he like? Is he an asshole?"

She shakes her head. "No."

"Has he ever done you wrong?"

"Never."

"Does he tell you how he feels?"

"He did."

"And you don't..." I clear my throat, almost getting choked up. "You don't feel the same?"

She hesitates, but then looks me straight in the eye. "I love him."

I know you do.

You told me last night.

But this doesn't feel like love.

Why wouldn't you just talk to me?

"Whoa!" Dex playfully slaps the table in front of him. "You didn't tell me you loved the guy."

Shaking my head, I continue. "Yeah so, I fail to see the problem here, Ror. If he loves you and you love him, then what's stopping you from just being happy?"

Maybe that came out sort of strong but dammit, the more she pulls back and fights what we have the more I fear I'm truly going to lose her.

"I need some fruit," she announces before slipping out of the booth, completely ignoring my question. "Excuse me."

Of course, she's running.

What is she so fucking scared of?

Dex merely shrugs as he takes a bite of his hashbrowns. I watch Rory walk toward the buffet, my anxiety, my anger, and my fear growing with every step she takes.

"Well, I guess I'll fill that plate now then."

I leave the booth and follow in Rory's footsteps until I

reach the buffet. Grabbing a plate, I grab several different foods not giving a damn what they are, until I reach Rory near the fruit.

"What the fuck is going on, Ror?" I murmur next to her so no one else can hear. "Are you really serious about this?"

"I'm sorry, Hawken."

My chest tightens as all the air leaves my body.

"Sorry? You're sorry? That's all you have to say?"

"I love you, Hawk. I do. But I can't do this to Dex. It will eat him alive if anything ever happens to us."

"So that's it then? You're walking away...just in case?"

"Please don't make this harder than it already is."

"Why? Because all the men in your life have always used you to get to Dex, choosing him over you?"

"Hawk—"

"Or because now you've gotten yourself so fucking twisted about it that now *you're* choosing him over being genuinely happy with someone. A man who loves you more than anything. A man who would give his fucking life for yours if he needed to?"

She stops dead in her tracks and stares at me in horror as if I've just slapped her across the face, her eyes glistening, chin quivering.

Shit.

That was harsh.

I didn't mean it.

I mean...I sort of did, but...

Fuck.

I just made it worse.

"Rory, I—"

"I need to pack."

"Ror..."

She sets her bowl of fruit down on the tray behind us and walks out of the restaurant frustratedly wiping her hands across her cheeks. I want to run after her. I could run after her, but doing so would certainly let Dex know something is going on between us and if I've learned anything from the past several minutes being in her presence, it's that Rory isn't ready for him to know anything. All I can do at this point is stand here and watch her walk away.

Fucking. Hell.

"What was that all about?" Dex asks when I reach the table and take the seat across from him. I scoop a hefty spoonful of eggs into my mouth and shake my head. "She said she wasn't hungry anymore and wanted to go pack."

Dex frowns. "What did you say to her?"

Shit.

"Nothing. She said she didn't want to talk about it anymore and needed to pack. I told her I would help if she needed it but she said no."

"Hmm." Dex's brows narrow. "She's not usually this upset over a guy. I mean, this is the first I've heard of her having feelings for someone in a long time."

Trying to help her lie along, I tell him about her date a while back. "Actually, she had a bad date at the beginning of playoffs. Showed up at my door crying about it one night."

"What? What the hell? Why didn't you tell me?"

I shrug like it's no big deal, even though to me it was a huge deal. "It wasn't an emergency or anything. She knew I lived close and some douche was using her to get to you so she bolted. Apparently, it happens a lot."

"So, what did you tell her? What did you do?"

"I invited her in and we watched porn, Dex." I roll my eyes. "What do you think we did? I made her some chocolate milk and we watched *Ted Lasso*. She just needed a safe space to cry it out and I was home. You remember I live basically next door, right?"

I won't mention that the porn thing actually happened if only for a minute.

Dex sips his coffee, processing what I've told him. "I guess I should thank you for being around," he says quietly. "I know my moving away probably hasn't been the easiest on her. We used to talk a lot but with Tatum and Summer I guess I just—"

"It's no bother, man. Rory and I are friends. I don't mind her being around at all."

In fact, my world is better when she's in it.

And I'm in love with her.

And I want to tell you that so fucking bad so I can fix whatever this is.

But I refuse to make it worse for her.

There's nothing I can do now.

I'm forced to let her decide what she truly wants.

"Hey lover-bros." Quinton smirks as he struts up to our table. "What's for breakfast?"

Dex smiles. "Your mom, asshole."

"My mom's asshole?" He laughs and pats his stomach. "What a rare delicacy. I hope it tastes like peaches."

Rain drips down my face as the resort comes back into view from the beach. This run wasn't half as therapeutic as I thought it might be, but I needed to get away by myself for a while. I can't even say I needed to clear my head because right now it's anything but clear. My entire body is a cluster fuck of confusion, anxiety, anger, and grief right now. Somehow while I was asleep overnight I lost the best thing to ever be in my life and I have no idea how I'm supposed to go about getting her back.

I don't know what's going on in Rory's head and I don't know how to make her see any differently, but it's gutting me that she's upset and hurting and alone right now. It's killing me that she won't even talk about this with me, that I have no say whatsoever.

I hate that I've spent the last few months hiding parts of my life from my best friend. I hate that Rory has done the same thing. She's always been close with Dex and now... fuck.

Because of what we did and how we've handled things, this could drive a wedge between them for years.

Soaking wet, I head upstairs and into the shower before I start packing for our flight home. This was supposed to be a celebratory vacation. The one where Rory and I finally got together and told Dex we're in love. Instead, I'm a fucking mess of emotions and want nothing more than to go home and hide out in my own apartment away from everyone for a while.

Knock, knock, knock.

Anticipation shoots through my chest.

Rory?

Maybe she finally wants to talk.

Maybe we can work this out.

There must be away.

But Rory's is not the face on the other side of the door when I open it.

"What do you want?"

Quinton purses his lips. "As I suspected. I'm not the person you thought would be knocking on your door, huh?"

I don't bother giving him an answer to that question. The fact he even asked tells me he already knows what's going on. I simply go back to folding my clothes, and by folding I mean wadding them up and throwing them in my suitcase.

"What do you want, Shay?"

He steps further into my room. "Are you okay?"

"Do I look fucking okay?"

"Not even a little bit, man."

"Well, aren't you the super sleuth."

"Hey, look," he says. "I didn't come here to make jokes or give you a hard time."

"Then why are you here?"

"Because I was in the elevator earlier when Rory stepped inside and she was a hot mess."

And there goes my heart...shattering a little bit more.

"Yeah."

He nods. "Yeah. Uh, she asked if she could sit with me on the plane. Of course, I said yes because she doesn't know I know that you two—"

"We're not."

"Not what?"

"We're not..." I flail my arm out to the side. "I guess we're not...anymore. Whatever we were, we're not now."

"Oh." He bows his head. "Can I ask what happened?"

I huff. "Hell, if I know, man. Last night was...fuck, it was an amazing night with her and at breakfast this morning she was crying to Dex about guy trouble and how she doesn't think it can work."

"Fuck..."

"Yeah. Fuck."

"Listen, I can tell her I can't s—"

"No. Don't do that," I tell him, shaking my head. "She obviously doesn't want to sit with me and it's fine. I don't want her to be uncomfortable."

"Do you think whatever's going on is fixable between you two?"

I toss my last shirt into my suitcase and then plop down on my bed. "Yeah, if Dex knew what was going on. I think if I just came out and told him the truth I could get him to help me convince her this would all be okay. That I love her fiercely."

His brows peak. "Wow. I think this is the first time I've heard Hawken Malone say he loves someone."

"Yeah well..." I take a deep breath and sigh. "It's always been her."

He takes a seat in a nearby chair. "Really? You really love her?"

"Have you ever loved someone, Quinton?"

He bobs his head. "Once. Years ago. There was a girl. And I thought she was my everything."

"What happened?"

"She met a bigger celebrity who showed interest in her and left me standing on a red carpet all by myself." He huffs. "So maybe I've never really been in love. Part of me isn't even sure love exists. My sister used to say it wasn't practical to fall in love." He laughs. "Of course, now she's married with two kids living in Hawaii, sooo..."

"I guess people change, eh?"

Quinton nods. "It's possible, sure. We all change as our lives change. Does Rory love you?"

"She says she does, but how do you love someone and walk away from them like nothing you ever did with that person meant anything? How do you walk away without a word? That's not love. To be perfectly honest, I don't know what the fuck to think anymore."

He leans forward and brings a hand to my knee. "For what it's worth Rory's a great girl. I'm sure she's scared. If you've always been relatively close, this is a big boundary to cross."

"Dude, we crossed all those boundaries long before this trip. We've crossed them more times than I can count."

Visions of Rory sprawled across her yellow chair float through my mind.

"Yeah but those aren't the boundaries I was talking about," Quinton explains. "Sex is the easy part. Making things official is the hard part. Saying yes throws her into the public eye because of who you are. And as much as you might not think it will have an effect, if you two were to get serious enough, it could very well change your relationship with Dex. You wouldn't just be his best friend anymore. Rory would be the most important person in your life. Your family."

"I know that," I blurt. "It's what I want. I want that with her. I want it all."

"But does she?"

"Fuck!" I cradle my head in my hands. "I don't know."

Quinton is quiet for a minute or two, allowing me the moment to sit in my own feelings.

"So, what do I do?"

"I think you should talk to Dex."

I shake my head. "I can't do that to her, Quinton."

"Why not?"

I cringe. "You should've seen her face this morning, letting me know Dex has no clue. She was begging me not to say anything. I can't betray her now. I won't do that to her. I need her to know she can trust me."

"Valid." He nods. "You're too much of a nice guy, Malone."

"Tell that to Rory, will you?"

"I think she knows, man. But you know if there's anything I can do, I'm here."

"Thanks. I appreciate you."

"Sure thing. I guess I should get my own shit packed huh?"

"Wheels up at four."

He stands from his chair. "Alright then. You going to be alright?"

"Yeah. Eventually."

20

RORY

We just lifted off the ground in Florida and already it feels like this plane is caving in on me. Quinton was nice enough to let me sit next to him so I don't have to spend the next few agonizing hours next to Hawken. At this point, I'm relatively sure it would be unbearable for both of us. I didn't want to hurt him. He's never been anything other than one hundred and ten percent in my court any time I've ever needed him. He put up with my stupid idea of being friends with benefits.

God, how dumb could I be?

This is all my fault.

And the worst part is, Hawk is right.

I am choosing Dex over my own happiness.

I am worried about how he would react.

I am worried about his future.

Hockey is his life.

This team is his life.

How can I not respect that?

Trying not to cry, as we're only a few seats away from

Hawk and Dex and Tate, I spend my time looking out the window, occasionally wiping my eyes and trying not to sniffle too loudly. Out of the corner of my eye, I notice Quinton texting on his phone. A second later, mine vibrates in my hand.

QUINTON

Are you okay?

Without texting him back, I nod. He gives me a sympathetic smile because he knows I'm anything but okay, and then types something else out on his phone.

QUINTON

You know Hawk loves you more than anything right?

My eyes snap to him so fast I could give myself whiplash.

How the hell does he know what's going on?

Did Hawken tell the guys?

Fuck!

Did he tell Dex?

QUINTON

Relax. Your brother is clueless. But the rest of us may have pulled it out of Hawk a long time ago.

ME

How long ago?

QUINTON

After he kissed you.

ME

You've all known all this time?

QUINTON

Uhh...yeah. And in his defense, he tried
awfully hard not to tell us. He didn't want
to. But we can be quite persuasive.

ME

I guess I'm not surprised.

QUINTON

Look, this is none of my business but for
what it's worth, I think you two can figure
this out. I think Dex would be okay with it.
And if he isn't, you know we would all
stand behind you and tell Dex to pull up
his big-girl pants and get over it, right?

A fresh flow of tears falls down my face. I'm so fucking
torn on the right decision between what my heart wants
and what is practical in my head.

ME

I don't know what to do, Quinton. My
brain feels like mush and my heart is
breaking. I don't want to hurt him but I
have.

QUINTON

I would love to tell you I have all the
answers to make this all better for you,
but I don't. My last love left me for
someone richer and more famous, so I'm
too jaded to give you expert advice. But if
I know one thing, it's that your brother has
grown up a lot in the past year. If he can
handle delivering his own kid, he can
handle a serious sibling conversation.

ME

Thanks Quinton.

I wipe my eyes for the thousandth time. Quinton wraps an arm around me and pulls me to his side, allowing me to have a quiet uninterrupted cry in the comfort of a sympathetic friend. And I do just that, until my eyes finally close, not to be opened again until the plane has pulled into the gate.

It's been almost two weeks since we got back from Key West with no word from Hawken. No surprise visits. No text messages. Nothing except for the now dying vase of flowers he sent the day after we got back with a note that says, *"I'll always choose you."*

I know this is all my fault, but that doesn't make it hurt any less.

I haven't left the house in days and haven't talked to anyone other than a few text exchanges between friends. It's been a quiet week. I've read six different books, baked banana bread, zucchini bread and a few dozen apple turnovers, and binged an entire season of *Married at First Sight*. I've eaten my weight in junk food one day and gone without eating anything the next, stared out the window more times than I can count, and even contemplated getting a cat to keep me company. I think I've showered maybe three times total and I've cried myself to sleep more often than not, including daytime naps. I've worn my favorite Hawken Malone jersey every day this week, immersing myself in his scent for as long as humanly possible, switching out my pajama pants each day.

Yesterday I wore pink ones with tacos all over them.

Today, they're green with highland cows.

I'm grieving the end of a relationship that never officially started. Or maybe I'm just kidding myself. Even though I didn't want to admit it to myself at the time, every part of me belonged to Hawken the moment he kissed me that night in my living room. He made every one of my young adult dreams come true. My crush finally saw me. Noticed me. Liked me. Wanted me.

Kissed me.

Told me I was his and he was mine.

He loved me.

Scratch that. He loves me.

Wants me.

Chooses me.

And I walked away.

I chose Dex.

Because Dex is safe.

Dex doesn't break my heart.

He doesn't use me.

Not that Hawken has ever done any of those things. He hasn't. But every time I allow myself to think about what life with him could be like, the young woman inside me who is used to being hurt by men tells me it's not a question of if...but when.

After pulling my next read off the shelf in my living room, I'm just about to order a sandwich from the deli around the corner when my phone dings with a text.

Speak of the Devil.

> **DEX**
>
> 911! I need you. Tatum needs you. How fast can you get here?

"Oh god," I gasp. "Please don't let it be the baby."

She and Charlee and Carissa are all about eight to twelve weeks pregnant. While the news gave us a cause for celebration in Key West, it's a scary time for all of them. Pregnancies can go south at any time for any reason and the thought of one of them having to endure that kind of pain and loss breaks my heart. Not giving a damn that I look like a complete troll, I grab my keys and purse and head out the door.

> **ME**
>
> I'm on my way! Is she okay?

Dex doesn't answer my text, which makes me uneasy. My lead foot taking over, and I make my way out of the city as fast as possible to get to their house on the lake. When I pull up, there are several cars parked on their driveway, each of them belonging to the guys on the team. I would recognize them anywhere.

"Oh fuck. This is serious," I murmur to myself as a larger black vehicle screeches to a halt behind me, effectively blocking me in. My heart drops if only for a second as I watch Hawken practically jump out the driver-side door.

I swing my car door open and climb out just as he reaches me. "Wha-what are you doing here?" His eyes sweep over my whole body, my unbrushed hair in a knot at the top of my head, my black-rimmed reading glasses on my face with his jersey and my cow pants. I know.

"I know, alright. I'm America's next top model. What the hell is going on Hawken?"

He shrugs as we both make our way to Dex and Tatum's front door. "Hell, if I know. The team got a nine-one-one and when that happens we drop everything."

Not wanting to be alone with him long enough to bring up whatever it is we're going through at the moment, I push their front door open. "Dex! Tate?"

Tatum shouts back, "In the kitchen, Ror!"

My brows knit.

She doesn't sound like she's in despair.

I swiftly move through their house until I reach the kitchen and stop short, my jaw hanging open. Glancing around the room, I spot Carissa and Colby first, followed by Milo and Charlee who is holding my beautiful niece. Quinton and Zeke are seated on the barstools at the kitchen island and every single one of them has a drink in their hands, some of them nearly empty. They've clearly been here for some time.

"What the fuck, Dexter?" I flail my arms out to the side almost hitting Hawken who follows behind me.

Dressed in a bright pink Hawaiian shirt and a pair of swim trunks, Dex takes a swig from the beer bottle in his hand and then cocks his head.

"What?"

Before I can say another word, his brow furrows as he takes me in and then asks, "What the hell are you wearing?"

"You..." I huff, blowing a piece of loose hair from my

face. "You called a fucking nine-one-one for Christ's sake. You said Tatum needed me!"

"I do need you babe," she answers. "You want a beer?"

"Do I want a..." I shake my head, staring at them like they've all gone fucking crazy.

"You want to tell me what the hell is going on that I just busted my ass to get here as fast as I could? I thought Tate was..." I stop, pinching my nose and trying to calm myself down. "I thought Tate had lost the baby."

Her face grows serious. "Aww, no Ror." She pats her tummy. "Baby is good. Just had an ultrasound yesterday. "

I turn to Dex, my eyes cold as I stare him down and wait for an explanation.

"We're all waiting too, Rory," Charlee says. "He told everyone to get here. We've just been waiting for you two."

I turn slightly to see Hawken step out from behind me and then turn back in a huff. "Well, we're here now so what is it?"

Dex takes another sip of his beer and then leans over the kitchen island in my direction, gesturing between me and Hawken.

"Well, I was just hoping you guys might be able to shine some light on why the two of you aren't fucking anymore?"

Pause everything.

Because when I say all the air leaves the room in this moment, I mean it.

All.

The.

Air.

Is.

Gone.

And.

I.

Can't.

Breathe.

A quick survey of the room tells me nobody else here knew that's what was going to come out of Dex's mouth. Charlee and Carissa's eyes are bulging and the guys are cringing.

"I knew you guys should've talked this out," Quinton murmurs, wiping his fingers across his forehead. My eyes meet Quinton's and he shakes his head, his hands up in defense.

"Wasn't me."

Son of a fucking bitch!

Hawken?

I turn on the spot and give him a pained expression, my cheeks flushing in embarrassment, but he shakes his head too.

"Wasn't me either, Ror. I would never do that to you."

My breaths come in quick and shallow, I press my palm against my chest, anything to try to dull the panic and pain shooting through my body.

"How did...who..." My muscles tense as I fold my arms over my chest. "How did y—"

Dex laughs. "Do you really think I didn't have you two figured out a long fucking time ago?"

What?

Hawken stands next to me but doesn't say a word. When I brave a glance his direction he looks equally perplexed.

"You two have had eyes for each other for years," Dex begins. "Honestly I'm shocked it's taken you this long."

I shake my head. "Dex, what on earth are you—"

"Do you think I don't realize when my best friend is having the best sex of his life?" he asks me with a smirk. Lifting his hand, he counts with his fingers. "His game is better. His workouts are more intense. He's in a lighter mood. He walks around like he can conquer the fucking world, but you know his biggest tell?"

Speechless, I merely shake my head. "His biggest tell is you, Ror."

Dex works his way around the counter until he's standing in front of me.

"Hawken Malone is one of the best goddamn hockey players I've ever had the pleasure of knowing and for the past several months, he's only had eyes for you."

Though we're not touching, I can feel Hawken's shoulders fall. I don't know why it seems like he's letting his guard down now, because inside, I'm holding mine up with both hands as my brother pounds against it like the Hulk.

My eyes beginning to water, I almost choke on my words. "That's not true."

"The fuck it isn't," Dex argues. "Do you remember that night at our housewarming party? When you blew up at me over fucking code pink?"

I remember it well, but I don't answer him.

"Who was it that ran after you when you got mad and walked away, huh?"

Hawken.

My emotions getting the better of me I blink, releasing a few tears down my cheek.

"Who keeps chocolate sauce in his refrigerator just for you because he knows you like chocolate milk even though he's not a fan?"

Hawken.

"Who came to your aid in no time when you asked for his help with your school's festival even though Colby and Zeke were already there?"

Hawken.

Fuck.

Dex cups my face in his hands, drying some of my tears with his thumbs. "And do you know how I know my best friend is madly in love with you?"

Sniffling, I shake my head.

"Because never in all my life have I ever seen him purposely take a penalty for the sole purpose of sitting in the sin bin, but he did it...for you, Rory. He was so fucking shaken up over you getting hurt, he did what he had to do to get close to you and make sure you were okay." He shakes his head. "I've never seen a hockey player do something like that in my entire fucking life. I've also never seen him so scared." His eyes narrow and he cocks his head. "Well...except for that night in the hotel when he hid you in the shower. That was a good one."

There's a bit of laughter around the kitchen from the guys, but even Hawken turns toward Dex, his jaw dropped in shock. Dex shrugs it off with a laugh. "She's the only one who wears that kind of perfume, dumbass. And she's worn it for years. I smelled it the moment you opened the door."

Hawken frowns. "Why didn't you ever say anything?"

"Because I was trying to give you the opportunity to tell

me your goddamn self, asshole." He teasingly punches Hawken's arm.

"Dex," I cry. Full-on tears now. "I'm so sorry."

He shakes his head, perplexed. "Tell me why. Why are you sorry? Are you sorry you slept with my best friend?"

"No." *Sniffle.*

"Are you sorry you fell in love with him?" He leans in and whispers, "You are in love with him, right?"

I nod. "Yes."

"Then what the hell do you have to be sorry for, Rory? Because the way I see it, you told me months ago right here in front of everyone that if you wanted to fuck every guy on our team, I wasn't to say a word. You told me I don't get to dictate who you see or don't see. That I don't get a say because you don't answer to me."

"I didn't mean i—"

"And you were right," he concedes. "You were right to put me in my place, Ror. I needed to be reminded that you're your own person and you're fully capable of finding your own happiness. You've sacrificed so much for me over the years even when you didn't want to but you don't need to do it anymore. I'm happy. I'm content. And I want that for you too so what the hell are you doing right now?"

"I don't know!" I burst out in a sob. "I don't want you to ever have to choose between us, Dex. I don't want to be the reason anything goes badly for either of you."

"Why would I ever have to choose between you?"

"I...Dex, if something happens and we don't work out..."

He frowns. "Why wouldn't you work out?"

"I don't know! There could be any number of reasons."

"Name one," Hawken finally includes himself in our conversation, his hand folding over mine.

My mouth falls open as tears continue to stream down my face. I glance around the room again, all our friends watching on with piqued curiosity.

"I..." My lips and chin tremble and there's a tremor in my voice. "What if you don't like my cooking?"

"I've never not loved anything you've ever made," he states softly. "Try again."

I gasp for a breath, trying to control my sniffles. "What if you don't like children? Little humans are my world for nine months out of the year."

He squeezes my hand. "I love kids, Rory. I wouldn't even mind having some of my own someday. I told you that in Key West."

"What if I can't *have* kids?"

"We'll adopt. Next?"

"What if...What if our schedules just don't jive?"

"We're both busy people, Ror." He grabs my other hand. "And I know how much you love your students. I would never ask you to stop doing what you love."

"Yeah but what if..." Sniffle. I'm grasping at straws. "What if I dress like this every day and you can't stand it?"

Hawken gives me a loving smile. "I think you're adorable just like this, Lady Bug."

"Lady Bug?" Dex gives Hawken a questioning look but Hawken ignores him. He only has eyes for me.

Swallowing the huge lump of nerves in my throat, I look around the room for help from my friends, but the looks on all their faces tell me I'm talking myself in circles and they're just waiting for me to come to the right conclusion. They're waiting for me to realize that I can't find a fault with Hawken because there aren't any.

He's been my person for years.

And he wants me to be his.

Dex smooths his hand down my arm. "Ror, I know what's it been like for you in the past. I know the guys in your life have been total shitheads because of me. That's why I made that fucked up code pink rule in the first place. Because I didn't want anyone I knew personally to hurt you. But what I failed to realize was that the perfect person for you has been by my side all this time."

"So, you're not...mad?"

"Fuck no, I'm not mad!" He beams. "Are you kidding me? Rory, I have my own family now. I have Tatum and Summer and a future Foster Tot on the way. So, knowing two of the most important people in my life have found something in each other? Fuck, do you know how good that feels? I don't have to worry about you anymore, Ror." He gestures toward Hawken. "There's nobody better to keep you safe and happy and loved and cared for than this guy right here. And he loves the shit out of you."

Hawk squeezes my hand again and I turn to him, sobbing. My nose running, my shoulders trembling, my stomach in knots, my heart pounding.

"I'm so sorry, Hawk." I shake my head. "I didn't want to hurt you. You didn't deserve it." *Sniffle.* "I thought—"

"I know what you thought, Rory," he says with a calmness to his voice. "You were just trying to protect your brother."

Sniffle.

I nod, wiping my nose on my arm.

266

God, I'm a hot mess right now.

He smooths my hair back from my face and wipes my tears. "I understand and it's okay. Let it be my job to calm your fears when you have them. Because I love you. And I would do anything for you. You know that."

Sniffle.

"I do know."

Sniffle.

"Then hold my hand and be my person, Rory Foster. I don't want to be with anybody else. You're it for me. I choose you and only you."

Dex leans in, turning his hand over between us. "I mean...unless I need him for something."

Hawken smiles and pushes my brother's face out of the way. "Get out of here, asshat, and let us have our moment."

Dex winks at me and steps back, walking around the counter to put his arm around Tatum.

"Do you think we can call this water under the bridge and start over?"

My brows lift. "You want to start over?"

"Something like that," he answers. "But I want to start over together this time. With you and me in the same place."

"What does that mean?"

"I think you know what it means." He smiles. "Move in with me, Rory. Live with me. I want you with me."

There's a collective celebration around the room as Hawken leans forward and kisses my forehead.

"That's really what you want?"

"Of course," he tells me. "You make me a better, happier man, Rory."

"Can we get a cat?"

"You want a cat?"

I nod. "To keep me company when you're on the road."

He smiles. "I'll buy you all the cats if it means you'll say yes."

"I have a lot of...stuff." I cringe. "And it doesn't really match any of your...stuff."

"I don't give two shits what my home looks like, Lady Bug. As long as you're in it that's all that matters." He thinks for a moment and then adds, "Well maybe you and two other things."

"Oh? What are those two things?"

He leans down to kiss my lips and then whispers, "The yellow chair is definitely coming into the bedroom. And I'll be happy to make a special display case for The Hawk."

We exchange a knowing look with each other and I snort in laughter. "Wow, you really do love me."

His smile falters and he holds my face in his hands. "Always, Rory. Forever if you'll let me."

"I love you, Hawken."

"I love you too, Ror."

Dex rubs his hands together. "Good. Now that these two goofballs can get back to fucking again, who's hungry?"

"Stop right there, Dexter," I shout, my teacher finger at the ready to scold him.

His shoulders drop. "What now?"

I step over to the counter and grab his beer, guzzling the rest in his bottle and then I slug him as hard as I can in his stomach.

"Oomph! What the fuck was that?"

"That's for peeing in Hawken's hotel room while I

stood on the other side of the shower curtain you fucking twat-hole!"

The room erupts in laughter as Dex tosses his head back with a cackle. "Sorry-not-sorry, Sis. You're lucky I didn't decide to drop a deuce."

The end

Want more Hawken and Rory?
Visit my website for their exciting epilogue!
https://www.authorsusanrenee.com

Want more of the Chicago Red Tails?
Scroll on for an excerpt of Quinton Shay's story.

SAVING THE GAME EXCERPT

Quinton

"Dude, my love for you is like diarrhea," Hawken professes to Dex as he shoves a few more fries into his mouth to keep from laughing. "I just can't hold it in."

Clearing my throat, I pull Hawken's plate of fries away from him, grinning when he scowls at me as I slide the plate toward Dex. "Dexter I'm pretty sure your bromance boyfriend just said his love for you is shit."

Laughing, Dex grabs a few fries from Hawken's shared plate and tosses them in his mouth. "Trust me, I think I'm beginning to believe him. Chose my sister over me and everything."

"She's a lot prettier than you and what can I say?" Hawken shrugs. "She sucks my dick better than you do, man."

Dex frowns and throws one of his fries on the table. "Fuck. And I watched tutorials for hours and everything."

Zeke nudges Hawken's arm, chuckling. "He means porn, bro. He watched porn for hours."

"Listen Dex, I've got this all figured out," I tell him with confidence. Lifting the hem of my shirt, I hold it out for him. "Feel my shirt. Do you feel that?"

Dex reaches out and rubs the fabric between his fingers. "Yeah."

"That's boyfriend material right there, man." I wink at him. "Fuck Hawken. There's a new bromance in town." Instead of the French fries Hawken's been gnawing on, I pass Dex my plate of pretzel bites and beer cheese.

The guys laugh as Dex rubs his chin pretending to consider my proposal.

"I do enjoy a good cheese," he says. "And if the next round is on you, I might just have to take you up on the offer, Quinton. Be a good boy and I might even let you grab my ass once in a while."

I sigh like a lovesick teenager. "Be still my heart. Of course, the next round is on me." I stand from our booth. "Be right back."

I head to the bar and order Dex and I another round, saying hello to a few of the mingling fans from out of town who aren't used to seeing the team hang out in a public bar. Pringle's has been good to us for years so most of the regulars know this tends to be our hangout spot. Occasionally though, we get a few newcomers who are shocked to see us here. We're just grateful we have a safe place to hang out and be ourselves once in a while and the management does a great job of helping foster that kind of environment for us.

Cathy, the bartender, hands me my drinks and I thank

her turning to walk back to our booth when someone catches my attention.

"Yes. Quinton, Mom. His name is Quinton Shay."

My head turns toward the female voice when I hear my name. A woman seated at the bar talking on her cell phone. She's facing away from me so I can't see her face, but hearing my name always makes me take notice. My parents weren't going for normal when they picked my name. They couldn't just settle on Sean or Mike or Jeff. Nope. They had to decide on a unique name that always had me standing near the back of the line in elementary school. Quinton is definitely not a name you hear often these days.

"What do you mean what does he do? He's a famous hockey player. I told you that."

That's right babe. Just another famous hockey player.

"Oh yeah. He's a super great guy. Total dreamboat. The whole package," she says. My brows peaking in response as I stand behind her eavesdropping.

Well, well, well. Dreamboat huh? Maybe I'm getting' lucky tonight.

"I mean, his schedule is really busy, you know? With games and his charity work and all, so I don't get to see him every day but we've been together for about six months now."

My expression changes from amusement to shock and then right back to amusement.

Who the heck is this girl?

"Dinner?" She squeaks. "Umm, yeah. He might be able to do that."

I watch her from behind, my head tilted as I watch with curiosity. She brings a palm to her forehead. "I'll ask him but with short notice and all, you know...he might not be able to make it."

Wow.

This girl's got balls.

There's got to be a story here and I kind of want to know it.

For shits and giggles of course.

Noticing she's drinking the same thing I'm holding in my hand, I linger a bit to listen to the end of her conversation, ignoring Dex's request for another beer.

"Alright. I'll see him in the morning but uh, I'll text him tonight and see if he can make it...yeah. Okay. Bye, Mom."

She lays her phone down on the bar, takes a deep breath and then drains the rest of the drink in front of her. I know I could walk away from this. By all means I should walk away from this. Maybe it's just my lightened mood because of our upcoming break or maybe I'm straight up stunned by this woman's audacity because last time I checked, I'm not only very single, I haven't been on an actual date in years.

If the guys were to hear what just happened, they'd be egging me on to hit on the girl and have myself a fun night. Confidence is attractive in a woman and she surely has that, but something seems off the more I watch her. She's not joking with a friend. She's not texting someone else. Not talking to anyone else so what gives?

Why the lie?

She finally turns and when I see her face I know I've seen her somewhere before. She's dressed in a pair of jeans and an oversized sweater that hangs off her shoulder. Her black bra strap on display. Her dark brown hair is tied up in a messy bun, but it's the bandana bow that's making me scroll through my mental rolodex because I know I've seen this woman before.

I don't know what makes me to do it. Maybe sheer dumb curiosity but here I am walking over to her and sliding one of my beers in front of her?

No turning back now.

"So, we're meeting the parents, I hear?"

Her jaw hangs open when I slide into the seat next to her and she realizes who I am.

"Oh, my God!" She gives herself a face palm, a goofy smile on her face as she shakes her head. "I totally deserve this, don't I. This is what happens to people like me."

I take a sip of my beer and smile back at her. "People like you. Do you mean women who phone a friend and lie to them about dating hockey players?"

"Shit. You heard all that?"

I laugh this time. "Kind of hard to miss when I was standing just a couple feet away."

"Oh fuuuudge." She brings her hands up to her blushing cheeks. "I am sooo so sorry. God, you probably think I'm the biggest psycho." Her eyes brow into huge saucers. "I swear I'm not a stalker or anything."

"It's fine. Really," I tell her, mesmerized by her mossy green eyes. "Forgive me, but I feel like I know you from somewhere and I can't for the life of me figure out where. What's your name?"

She takes a sip the beer I gave her, part of me wanting to chastise her for accepting an open drink from a guy. I might be a famous hockey player but we're not all fine upstanding men. "Oh. I'm Kinsley Allen. I actually took pictures at Hawken and Rory's wedding in the arena."

"Yes!" I sit up taller, pointing my finger at her. "That's it. I remember now. Sorry I didn't recognize you in casual clothing."

She slouches, slightly rolling her eyes. "Ugh, I don't dress up anymore unless I absolutely have to."

You look perfect just as you are.

"Anymore?"

"My parents," she starts with an annoyed nod. "That's who I was talking to on the phone."

"Uh oh." I grin. "This doesn't sound good."

"If I tell you I grew up in L.A. where several celebrity families were our neighbors, does that give you any indication?"

"Ah, so you're a socialite." She narrows her eyes. "Ooor your parents are...or were?"

"In all honesty, I think my parents would scoff at the word socialite. They prefer words with a little more finesse."

I pass her a smirk. "So spoiled little rich girl doesn't describe you?"

She laughs. "Not hardly. I mean, if my parents had anything to say about it, I would be back in L.A. helping them run their empire and taking over when they retire, but their life is so far from what I want. That's why I moved here. Far away from them."

"Oh?"

"I've seen enough of that lifestyle to never want to be a part of it ever again."

"What?" I bring my hand to my chest pretending to be

dumbfounded. "You mean there are rich people in the world who do bad things? Surely not!"

She huffs out a light laugh. "If you only knew."

Interesting.

It's not every day you see someone who comes from money not want the life money can afford. Something about her demeanor draws me in though. Like she has layers I want to peel back one at a time as I get to know her.

"So you were talking to your parents. Does that mean you're flying home to see them or something?"

"No." She shakes her head with a cringe. "They're in town for a few days on business and they want to meet my rich boyfriend. Because far be it for me to date a normal guy who has a normal job and makes an honest normal wage." Realizing what she just said, she squeezes her eyes closed and cringes again. "Aaaand I just put my foot in my mouth. I'm sorry, I didn't mean to say that you don't—"

"I totally get it," I reassure her. "Professional hockey isn't exactly on the list of normal jobs with a normal wage."

"Right, but it sure as hell made my mom happy to hear I'm not an embarrassment to the family and found a celebrity athlete to date instead of a local plumber, though I'm not positive she believes me. Not that I care at all. I'll tell her anything to keep her off my back so I can live my life in peace."

"So can I ask you something then?"

"Sure. I mean, I've pretty much laid my entire life story out for you when you never really asked, haven't I?" She smiles. "Ask away."

"Why me?"

"What?"

"Why did you tell your parents you were dating me specifically."

"Uh…" She bites her lip to hide her nervous smile. "Because you're single aaaand not at all hard to look at." She winces. "Aaaand you were the first person to come to my mind probably because I saw your post-game interview on T.V."

She's cute when she blushes.

"Well, I like the honesty, so thank you, I guess."

"No, I should be thanking you," she says as she smooths a hand down my arm. Her simple touch causing me to suddenly think about what it would feel like to have her hands all over me. "For not getting someone to kick me out of this bar the minute you heard me tell my parents I'm dating you. I really am sorry and don't worry about a thing. I'll be telling them tomorrow that you caught a bug and can't make dinner."

I can't believe I'm doing this. "Or you could tell them I'm available."

She cocks her head. "I'm sorry?"

What the fuck am I doing?

"You said your mom probably doesn't believe you, so why not shove her disbelief in her face? It just so happens, I'm free."

"Wait," she says leaning back on her stool. "Are you seriously offering to be super petty with me to stick it to my parents and get them off my back?"

I laugh. "What if I told you my name was Quinton Petty Shay?"

Her eyes narrow. "Is it?"

"Not at all," I shake my head. "But this sounds like an

opportunity too fun to pass up. If you're going to lie to them about us being in a relationship, go big or go home, right?"

"You're serious?"

"One hundred percent. I've got a couple days off. If you're in, I'm in."

She considers it for a moment, an adorable smirk lighting up her face. I notice the cute dimple in her right cheek when she smiles. She really is quite pretty.

"Can we make up some crazy shit about how we met?"

"I wouldn't have it any other way," I tell her.

"Oh, my God, I can't believe I'm about to take you up on this kind of offer."

"Going once...going twice..."

"I'm in!" She laughs, taking another drink of her beer. "I'm so fucking in."

"Perfect. Let me give you my number and then you can text me the details."

"Okay. It'll probably be super upscale, if that's okay. My parents would never step foot in a place like this."

Typing my number into her contact list, I smile. "Don't worry. I'll wear a designer suit." I stand and she follows offering me her hand.

"It was really nice meeting you, Quinton Petty Shay."

I wrap her hand in mine, her skin soft and warm. I find myself not wanting to let go, but if I don't walk away, I may do something we'll both really regret tomorrow. "The pleasure was all mine, Kinsley."

She sees herself out and I head back to where the guys are seated, laughing about who knows what and who cares.

"Dude, where's my beer?" Dex asks when I lower my near empty glass to the table.

"Our bromance is over before it started Dexter. I'm giving all my fake love to someone else."

"Fake love? What are you talking about?"

"Does this have anything to do with Kinsley?" Hawken asks. "I saw you talking to her."

"Yeah," I nod sliding into the booth. "It does. She told her parents she was dating me."

The shocked expressions looking back at me makes me laugh. "She was lying, obviously. She just wanted her parents off her back so I offered to fuck with them with her because why the hell not?"

Zeke chuckles. "So, you're going to pretend to be her boyfriend?"

"Yup."

"Oh, fuck. This ought to be good."

Quinton and Kinsley's story releases January 11, 2024! You can PREORDER HERE now!

OTHER BOOKS BY SUSAN RENEE

All books are available in Kindle Unlimited

The Chicago Red Tails Series

Off Your Game – Colby Nelson

Unfair Game – Milo Landric

Beyond the Game – Dex Foster

Forbidden Game – Hawken Malone

Saving the Game – Quinton Shay

Bonus Game – Zeke Miller

Remember Colby's brother, Elias Nelson? Here's his story! A spinoff of my Bardstown Series of small town interconnected romances!

NO ONE NEEDS TO KNOW: Accidental Pregnancy

(Elias and Whitney's story)

(Bardstown Series Prequel – Previously entitled SEVEN)

I LOVED YOU THEN

The Bardstown Series

I LIKE ME BETTER: Enemies to Lovers

YOU ARE THE REASON: Second Chance

BEAUTIFUL CRAZY: Friends to Lovers

TAKE YOU HOME: Boss's Daughter

ROMANTIC COMEDIES

Smooch: Arya's Story

Smooches: Hannah's Story

Smooched: Kim's Story

Hole Punched

You Don't Know Jack Schmidt
(The Schmidt Load Novella Book 1)

Schmidt Happens
(The Schmidt Load Novella Book 2)

My Schmidt Smells Like Roses
(The Schmidt Load Novella Book 3)

CONTEMPORARY ROMANCE

The Village series

I'm Fine (The Village Duet #1)

Save Me (The Village Duet #2)

*The Village Duet comes with a content warning.

Please be sure to check out this book's Amazon page before downloading.

Solving Us

(Big City New Adult Romance)

Surprising Us (a Solving Us novella)

ACKNOWLEDGMENTS

I don't even know if people read these acknowledgements anymore so I'm going to use this as a bit of a diary entry, only you all, my readers, are my diary.

I wish I could explain to you all how much my life has changed in the last two months. I won't get into the "dirty details" because I know everyone has a story, but I need you to understand how sincerely grateful for ALL of you, I am.

When I released *Beyond the Game* (*Dex and Tatum's story*) back in June I had NO idea it would blow up to become the story it is. In fact, if I recall, I told you all that I was worried it wasn't the story everyone would love.

But you all proved me so very wrong.

I woke up one morning in early July and posted a Tiktok about the book and it went sort of viral (maybe about 10K views) and I thought nothing of it other than I expected a few more Kindle Unlimited page reads than normal. That same morning a reader on my team posted a random video I knew nothing about...until it blew up and she was excited to tell me about it.

Holy shit!

I did NOT expect what followed!

Everything began to snowball that day.

People were actively buying my book(s) and talking

about them. *Beyond the Game* climbed the charts over the next twenty-four hours until it hit #1 in categories in several different countries and was within the top 100 in the entire Kindle store! The Chicago Red Tails have also been offered an audiobook deal and they're in production right now! Every single one of the goals I set for myself this year has been smashed! July was by far the best month of my eight-year career and as I watched everything happen I cried over, and over, and over, and over again.

Because you see, I didn't start this job with thousands of dollars to invest. I'm a happily married mom of two kids, two dogs and a cat in rural Ohio. We live a pretty normal life (I mean as normal as a "smutty" romance writer can lead) but if you knew our story, you would understand why this forward movement in my writing career means THE WORLD to us. We spent years trying to keep our heads above water. Tear-filled nights wondering how we were going to make it. Scared we wouldn't be able to give our kids the life they deserved.

The life we wanted to be able to give them.

We haven't purchased a new mattress for our bed in over sixteen years. We're still sitting on the same two couches we bought after getting married twenty years ago. (Don't get me started on the amount of pet hair, and drool and little baby vomit is probably caked into those suckers). We drive two cars from 2006. Both literally falling apart (no really...one is duct taped on the bottom so you can't see the road from the passenger seat!)

I know these are first world issues and we are blessed beyond measure and please know I'm not saying these things for sympathy. Quite the opposite. I hope you can read these words and know how unbelievably grateful I am for all of you. In one month, you've changed my life for good! Without you all reading my books, I wouldn't be in the place I am right now to FINALLY be able to fix some of these "old" problems for my family. And I can stand proud and know that what I do is helping my family by leaps and bounds.

It may not last. This could all go away tomorrow and that's fine, but because of all of you, because of you downloading my books, reading them, sharing them, and talking about them, you have made SO MANY of my dreams come true. YOU DID THAT! THANK YOU, THANK YOU, THANK YOU!

You might think you're just reading a book, but PLEASE know you're doing so much more. You're blessing the lives of those who put in the hours and the tears and the uncertainty while writing the stories you love to read.

I love you all so very much.

Special Thanks to my Patreon subscribers for sticking with me in so many aspects of my writing process!
Katie Powell
Dawn Bryant
Betsy Chapman
Lindsay Brewer

Interested in joining my Patreon
or learning more about it?
Click HERE!

ABOUT THE AUTHOR

Susan Renee wants to live in a world where paint doesn't smell, Hogwarts is open twenty-four/seven, and everything is covered in glitter. An indie romance author, Susan has written about everything from tacos to tow-trucks, loves writing romantic comedies but also enjoys creating an emotional angsty story from time to time. She lives in Ohio with her husband, kids, two dogs and a cat. Susan holds a Bachelor and Master's degree in Sass and Sarcasm and enjoys laughing at memes, speaking in GIFs and spending an entire day jumping down the TikTok rabbit hole. When she's not writing or playing the role of Mom, her favorite activity is doing the Care Bear stare with her closest friends.

facebook.com/authorsusanrenee

x.com/indiesusanrenee

instagram.com/authorsusanrenee

tiktok.com/@authorsusanrenee

amazon.com/author/susanrenee

goodreads.com/susanrenee

bookbub.com/authors/susan-renee

patreon.com/RomanceReadersandWishfulWriters

Printed in Great Britain
by Amazon